Chapter One

Talia bent over and rested her hands on her knees, gasping for breath, her sun-kissed blonde hair almost reaching the ground. Mother would not be happy with her for ditching her escort, but being twenty-one meant she shouldn't need a guard to travel the fifteen-minute walk to her cousin's manor. Plus, Tatum was sixty-five years old. If they'd really expected trouble, they wouldn't have assigned her such an old man.

Helm was a safe kingdom, a place where children played in the woods for hours, where people didn't lock their doors, where neighbors trusted neighbors.

On her walk, she'd wound in and through yards so Tatum would have no clue where she went, and she lost him at least a half mile ago. Talia shouldn't have ditched him. She loved the man, a sweet grandfatherly type who often teased her, but she didn't need an escort.

The light breeze ruffled the leaves above her, and she stared into the green canopy bearing multitudes of shiny red apples. She and Maisy should make an apple

WHEN THE FOREST CRIES

pie this evening. Her cousin's specialty was desserts, and they could throw together a pie in no time. They'd eat that delectable treat in no time too.

Talia's mouth watered thinking about the sugary cinnamon sweetness. Can't forget a scoop of ice cream, either.

A gust of air swept a branch from the apple tree towards her, and she reached up and wrapped her fingers around a red waxen surface. She twisted the apple around and found not one bruise on its skin.

She shouldn't be thinking about taking somebody else's apple, but it was just one apple, and it was sure to be a juicy treat. She glanced around.

The trees partially hid a ramshackle hovel at the back of the property, but nobody seemed to be outside either there or at the house next door, and tons of massive leafy apple trees filled the yard. They wouldn't miss one.

Talia plucked the apple from the branches. When she returned home, she'd send an anonymous gift to the tree-owner, perhaps a basket of fine wines or some specialty spices most in the kingdom didn't have access to.

She bit into the apple, and a light, fresh aroma filled her nose, and a crisp, sweet taste met her tongue. She savored the flavor as she slowly chewed what must be a new variety of apple she'd not yet had. Father must buy some of these seeds to plant at the castle gardens.

A buzzing noise filled her ears, as if a thousand cicadas circled her, and the wind whipped her blonde mane around. She stood in the middle of a swirling vortex, the greens and blues and browns of the world blurring together. A wooziness swam through her head, and her body swayed.

Then the noise, the motion, the wind gusts all disappeared.

Talia placed her hand on the rough bark of the apple tree to steady herself. A wave of sadness swept through her, a queasiness in her tummy. Hopefully, she wasn't coming down with an illness.

A flicker of movement in the distance caught her eye, a hawk soaring down around a sky-high brick tower, its screech carrying through the still air.

Wait, what? There'd been no tower there moments before, only the small cottage.

A sizable home in the same reddish-brown brick sat adjacent to the tower. Talia shaded the bright sun from her eyes and slid her gaze up the wall but couldn't see the top. No windows, either.

"Well, what do we have here?" a woman cackled as she traipsed down the stone path in a long red dress, a deep purple cape flapping behind her and a long braid

WHEN THE FOREST CRIES

hanging down her back. The thick silvery braid with black strands shimmered in the sunlight, but her smile was not bright. "An intruder, I see."

Her gleaming eyes took Talia in from head to toe. Despite the hot sun, a shiver flowed through Talia's body, and she wiped her clammy hands on her jade linen dress. The urge to run overtook her, but she remained where she stood. She must at least apologize for trespassing.

"I'm sorry. I wandered into your yard by accident, but I'd best be on my way." Talia turned to leave.

"Unfortunately, you'll be staying for a while. Justice must be served." The woman flashed an impish grin, but beyond it was a chilling strength.

The blood in Talia's veins turned ice cold, and she rushed for the house next door. "My parents are expecting me. I really must go." She was so close that she could see the home, the children and mother coming out their front door.

"You stole my apple." The razor-sharp words snapped Talia still.

"I didn't steal anything. I—" A wetness leached into her skin, and she stared at the mushy apple in her hand, the bright red skin now a mottled brown, and the fleshy insides black. A worm wriggled out of a hole, and the smell of decay filled her nose.

SUZI WIELAND

"The proof is in your hand, you half-wit," the woman growled, and the apple tumbled from Talia's grasp to the ground, exploding into a poof of black powder.

What was going on? Was the apple drugged? Had she fallen asleep and was having a nightmare? She shouldn't have left Tatum behind.

"My father is—" The king. But this woman would take advantage of him. "My father will compensate you for this apple. I apologize for taking it without asking."

"It's too late." The woman grimaced at her pointy boot and rubbed a spot of dirt off the side.

Talia took off for the house on the other side of the trees, her legs pumping. A few more short yards, and she'd be safe from the loon behind her. Talia's body slammed into something hard and solid, and she bounced backwards, her head thunking the ground.

What the bejesus? She sat up, a bit dazed, and rubbed her eyes. No obstacle was in her way. No tree, no wall. Her head pounded, but she had to escape this woman. Talia jumped to her feet and sprinted off, but once again whacked into something unseen.

Her fingers met the rough and scratchy bark of a tree. Except there was no tree in front of her. She felt around, but it extended up and to the sides.

WHEN THE FOREST CRIES

"Help," she cried to the woman and her children playing in the yard next door, but they didn't look up. "Help me, please," Talia screamed. She pounded on the invisible tree or wall or whatever it was with her fist.

But there was no noise... nothing. And she only came away with a scratched up hand.

And the laughter of the woman behind her.

"Nobody can hear you," she spat. "Holler all you want."

Talia slowly turned around to the imposing woman. Her face showed the age of Talia's grandmother, but her expression was hardened, not light and airy as Nana's. The dress was one of wealth and not a small cabin on the outskirts of town.

Talia looked again to the large brick home shrouded by trees, the grand tower rising to eternity. The hairs on the back of her neck rose. "Who... who are you?"

"Such an impertinent girl. I will expect better from now on." The woman huffed. "I am your new employer, but you can call me Zella."

Chapter Two

New employer? The woman was crazy.

Zella stalked away, and Talia tried to make a run for it again—there had to be an opening in the invisible wall, but her feet started parading through the long grass after Zella as if they had a mind of their own. She grunted in an effort to stop, but the house got closer and closer.

Zella was a witch.

Growing up, Talia had heard stories about witches from the adult folk, but she always thought the myths were meant to keep children from wandering off. Her lip trembled as Zella forced her to march. The witch was taking her inside and would cook her and eat her, or feed her to the wolves.

"Please let me go. I'm begging you. My father will pay you—" Talia's march halted, and Zella sneered at her.

"Quiet, you sniveling thief."

WHEN THE FOREST CRIES

"Please don't eat me. I don't have much meat on my bones, and I probably don't taste very good."

"Enough drama." Zella threw her hands up and spun around. "As if I don't get enough of that around here." She continued towards the house, and Talia's feet trotted behind her, but not of her own will.

Talia snagged a low branch on a passing tree and held on for dear life, but the branch ripped out with a snap. Zella sprung around, her wide eyes darting from the tree to the cracked branch on the ground to Talia. Then to the tree.

"You're lucky nothing happened to my apples." She scowled and headed off.

Talia frantically searched the yard for someone…anyone…but saw no sign of her escort or anybody else, and soon they reached the house. The air was cooler, the sun not as bright, and Talia craned her neck to look at the round tower blocking out the sun. She couldn't see the top.

Talia's feet carried her inside, and Zella waved her hand. The door slammed shut.

"Charlyn," Zella screeched. "Get your worthless butt down here." She strode down a hallway, with Talia following, and entered an elegant living room with fine furniture and shelves of glass bottles and other containers. Talia couldn't tell what was inside them though. Large windows framed by velvet drapes let in the sun, brightening the room immensely.

They proceeded to another smaller room filled with even more wall-to-ceiling shelves. Zella took her place behind a grand cherry wood desk, and Talia's feet stopped off to the side. A heavy book lay open, but Zella paid it no attention and dug in her drawer. She removed a quill, uncapped a small bottle, and began writing with a deep red ink on a piece of paper.

A woman about Talia's age hustled into the room, her thick auburn braid flying behind her.

"Yes, Zella?" She looked up with wide eyes.

Zella glanced at a clock on the wall. "I called you five minutes ago."

"Yes, I know, but I was in the middle of…" She noticed Talia standing there and frowned.

Zella followed Charlyn's gaze. "This is Talia. She is—"

"How did you know my name?" Talia was stunned. Did that mean Zella knew she was a princess?

"Did I speak to you?" Zella snapped, gripping her quill tightly. A drop of red ink fell to the paper, and Zella swiped her finger, removing most of the red but leaving a stain.

It almost looked like… blood.

WHEN THE FOREST CRIES

"I'm sorry." Talia shrunk back. Charlyn was giving her the evil eye, and Zella was about to bite her head off. She tried to remember the stories she'd heard about witches, but none of them ended well.

"I caught this girl stealing my apples, and now she needs to work off her debt."

"But I only had a couple of bites." And her father could pay for it.

"Do you know how much magic was contained in those two bites? How many years it's taken to grow that apple? Nobody appreciates hard work these days." Zella returned her focus to the paper and wrote out a few more lines while the two girls stood there watching. Finally, she laid down her quill and looked up.

"Sign this." Zella thrust the paper towards Talia. "It's our agreement about you working off your debt."

Talia mustered up her courage. Zella couldn't do this to her. "What if I don't?" She hadn't even read it, and she wasn't sure she wanted to.

"But you will." Zella smirked, and Charlyn let out a snort. Talia's feet carried her around the desk, and her hand lowered to the quill. "Hard work is good for the soul."

Talia fought the movement with all her might, but she was a marionette, and somebody else was controlling her.

SUZI WIELAND

"Okay." Talia had no choice, so she reached for the paper and scanned it quickly. "Three years? You expect me to work for you for three years for one little apple?"

Zella pounded her fist on the table, and Talia jumped. "That was a magic apple, and it will take me three years to replace it, so you darn well will be working for me for that time."

Talia felt her hand reaching for the quill again, and within a few seconds, her name was scribbled across the line. Zella smiled in satisfaction and signed below Talia's name.

Why was Zella even doing this? She was a witch, but she needed Talia to sign a paper? This didn't make sense.

Talia glanced out the window to see the rows of trees, their branches heavy with apples. The bark almost seemed tinted gray instead of the dark brown they usually were.

Zella cleared her throat. "You have been given a chance to make amends, but you will not grow if you do not learn. So take advantage of what I've given you."

She held the paper in her hands and blew on the ink. "Your duties are to assist Charlyn."

"I get an apprentice?" Charlyn gaped.

WHEN THE FOREST CRIES

"No, you ninny," Zella scoffed. "Apprentices do not have apprentices. She will not be learning magic. She'll take care of your other duties."

Charlyn's shoulders relaxed, and her grin grew a yard wide.

"What does that mean?" Talia asked.

"That you're the maid." Charlyn's head bobbed happily. "Thank you, Zella. You won't regret this. And now I can take more time to work on my spells."

Zella waved to the door. "Show her around the house. She will share a room with you."

"But there's—"

Zella glared at her.

"Yes, ma'am. I'll conjure another bed." Charlyn gave her an obviously forced smile.

"And tomorrow you will create clothes for her too." Zella tapped the end of the quill pen on her desk. "You need to work on that. I can't stock my store with the junk you're creating now."

"Of course." Charlyn sighed. Talia wanted to ask what store she was speaking of, but Zella flung the paper into a drawer and scowled at them.

"Now, get out of my office."

Talia followed Charlyn out, this time using her own feet. She'd pretend to do as asked, and as soon as everybody went to bed, she'd make her escape. There had to be a break in that wall somewhere.

Charlyn showed Talia around the first and second floors. The house was much smaller than her castle but as large as her cousin Maisy's house.

"Why is she making us share a room?" Talia asked after they passed the sixth bedroom. Being in the same room as Charlyn complicated things, and Talia would have to wait until the girl was asleep.

"Because she's Zella." Charlyn continued down the hall. "You'll be doing the laundry and cleaning and cooking our three meals a day. Breakfast is promptly at seven, lunch at one, and dinner at six."

Talia wouldn't have a problem with the cooking part—she'd hung out with the cooks at the castle plenty, and her mother had taught her to cook, but the cleaning was new to her.

What was she talking about? She wouldn't be around here tomorrow.

"What's in the tower?" Talia asked as they came down the steps to the main floor again.

"That's where we…" Charlyn glanced towards the closed office door. "It's where we do our magic."

"But Zella was doing magic earlier. Can you only do it in the tower?"

WHEN THE FOREST CRIES

"Don't be a simpleton." Charlyn sighed. "We can do magic anywhere, but it's where Zella processes her apples. Now go make lunch." She pointed to the kitchen.

Talia stepped through the doorway, and Charlyn took a seat at the table. "There's food in the cupboard."

"But what do I make?" What if Zella didn't fancy her food? Would she punish Talia?

"Anything you want," Charlyn said in a bored voice. "It doesn't matter."

"What do you mean?" Talia didn't want to anger Zella further.

"She'll just magick it into whatever food she wants anyway."

The idea was impressive, and Talia forgot for a moment that she was their prisoner. "Then why do I have to make anything?"

"Because we can't make something out of nothing. We can only take what's already made and change it. Now get the bread out for sandwiches." Charlyn spoke to Talia as if she was a small child.

Talia turned towards the cupboard. She had to try to get Charlyn talking to learn as much as possible about Zella so when she escaped, she'd be able to share with the world all she could about this nasty witch.

Chapter Three

Zella (and Charlyn too) magicked the food as Charlyn had predicted, but Talia was stuck eating the tasteless sandwich she'd made. There had been cooked chicken in the icebox, which was obviously kept cold by magic, but that was it. No butter or dressing and the chicken was blah, apparently cooked with no seasonings.

During lunch, Zella only spoke to Charlyn, questioning her on how her spells were going. And Talia spent the afternoon and evening doing laundry as Charlyn made up a grueling daily schedule for tomorrow. Work from morning until night. At least the last few hours would be spent in the kitchen, which wasn't so hard.

Thankfully, Talia wouldn't be around after tonight.

Talia set down a large basket of towels from the clothesline in the backyard. The table shifted underneath the weight, and Charlyn glared at her, quill in her hand and paper beneath it.

"Why don't you magick the laundry?"

WHEN THE FOREST CRIES

"Because hard work is good for the soul." Charlyn set down her quill. "Although, I'm pretty sure if I wasn't here, Zella would be using magic to take care of those things."

"So you're her servant?" Talia folded the towels as perfectly as she could.

"I am not." Charlyn huffed. "I have one more year on my apprenticeship, and after that, I can go out on my own. I'm ready now, but Zella thinks I need more work." She said the words in a mocking lilt that showed her true feelings.

Talia finished the last towel and set it on the pile in the basket.

"You can put those away, and then it's time for bed," Charlyn said.

Talia hefted the full basket on her hip, went upstairs to put the towels away, and returned to their shared room. A stunning purple and turquoise quilt covered the first bed, along with tasseled pillows, but the second bed had a thin brown blanket.

Charlyn pointed towards the door. "You can get ready in the washroom after I'm done, and then I'll take you to the library."

"What for?" Talia glanced at the window. It was still light outside, but the clock had said it was nine o'clock.

SUZI WIELAND

"For something to read, of course. Monday and Wednesday evenings are for expanding your world. You will not grow if you do not learn." Charlyn gave Talia a patronizing look. "Zella requires us to spend an hour reading before we go to bed."

"I can read books about magic?" Maybe Talia would learn some of Zella's secrets. She might sneak a book with her when she left.

"No. I read books on magic, but you won't. Zella has numerous books to choose from. I'm sure you'll find something."

Talia hid her disappointment as Charlyn went out the door. This was the first time Charlyn left her alone all day, but Talia must stick with her plan. Zella was downstairs anyway.

In a half hour, Talia was in her pajamas with a book in her lap. Zella's library had shelves and shelves of books, and Charlyn was right: Talia had no difficulties finding something to read. She couldn't focus on the words though because she was reviewing her plan in her head.

Going out the front or back door was too easy, and Zella might have a spell on the door to prevent Talia from leaving, or maybe a spell that would warn Zella someone was exiting.

Talia would go downstairs, crawl through the kitchen window, and quietly drop to the ground. She'd have plenty of time to get away. And really, Zella had probably hexed her earlier to make it seem as if there was a wall. She would be able to escape tonight.

The moonlight shone in the window because Charlyn preferred to sleep with the shutters wide open. She'd been sleeping for at least two hours, and Zella had to be out now too, so now was the time to go.

Talia threw off the thin, scratchy blanket and crept out of the hard bed, down the hallway, down the steps. The kitchen had the best windows, and she could climb on the counter to get out.

Talia opened the shutters and breathed in the fresh, crisp night air. Freedom was so close.

She scrambled out the window and closed the shutters. She weaved through the trees under the bright moonlight, constantly glancing at the windows. Charlyn had shown her which was Zella's room, and Talia checked for movements or light but saw none.

This was too easy.

SUZI WIELAND

Finally, she arrived at the edge of the property adjacent to the gravel road. Thank the heavens. Her parents would be so worried, along with her cousin, her aunt, and her uncle. They were probably out searching for her right now. She was surprised they hadn't knocked on Zella's door yet.

Talia stepped towards the road, but her foot hit something solid.

Oh no.

Her chest tightened, and she squeezed her eyes shut for a moment before reaching out.

Her fingers hit rough bark. It went all the way from the ground to as high as Talia could jump. She took a step, and the wall seemed to continue.

This wasn't possible.

She'd thought Zella had just hexed her earlier to keep her from leaving, but the wall was still there. She strode along the front of the property, keeping her hand on the rough surface. There had to be a hole somewhere.

She continued until she hit a corner and turned down the side. Walking, running, reaching all over. This was hopeless—Zella really had her trapped.

But no, she couldn't give up hope yet.

WHEN THE FOREST CRIES

She kept going around another corner, and then a third, and a fourth. And then she was back to where she started.

Talia fell to her knees, crying. She was really imprisoned here… for three years.

Away from her family, forced to be the maid for a horrible witch and her apprentice.

What would she do?

Chapter Four

Talia spent a fitful night of sleep in the hard bed. She'd never considered before how lucky she was to sleep on her comfy pile of blankets with her fluffy pillows.

A loud ringing blared through the room, and Talia opened her eyes to see it was six-thirty. Dawn had not yet arrived, and Talia yawned.

"Get up." Charlyn's tired voice cut through Talia's haze.

She dragged herself out of bed and to the washroom, and then downstairs to make breakfast for Zella. The kitchen, although smaller than the one at the castle, was sizable, with its large oven, plenty of counter space and cupboards, and a sizable icebox.

"Late night?" Zella dug into her food, a frustrating smirk on her face. "You'd better wake up. Today is a harvesting day."

She took a bite of her spinach quiche, which had been plain scrambled eggs before she spelled them. She chewed slowly before speaking to Charlyn. "This

WHEN THE FOREST CRIES

afternoon, I've set aside four hours. Make sure that the half-wit knows what she's doing so she doesn't bruise them. I'll be in my office."

"Yes, Zella," Charlyn replied in a bright voice.

The older witch turned her attention to Talia, a scowl marring her face. "If you bruise any more of my apples, then your stay will be much longer." The angry threat hung in the air, and Talia nodded morosely.

Zella swept out of the room, her silk burnt orange dress swishing. She looked as if she was attending tea.

Talia spent the morning scrubbing the washroom down, sweeping the floors, and making another meal. After they ate, Talia followed Charlyn to the front yard next to the stone path. Charlyn counted each tree on their way, and after stopping, took out a brown roll of paper, and unrolled it. A hand-drawn map filled the scroll, and Charlyn ran her finger down the paper and re-counted the trees until she got to the one they stood under.

"This is it," she said, staring towards the top of the tree filled with golden apples.

"Why are they yellow?" Talia asked. All the other apples in the yard were red.

"That means they're ready to harvest. You need to be gentle. Twist the apple to get it off and place it carefully in the basket. Do not drop them and do not

SUZI WIELAND

toss them. Unless you want to be here for a hundred years."

Talia squinted at the loads of apples in the tree and back to the basket. They would have to haul that basket up and down a lot.

"That'll take forever. Don't you have more baskets?"

Charlyn mumbled a few terse words and waved her hand in the air. The one basket multiplied into five. "I'll make more when we need them. Get on the ladder."

"What ladder?" The words were barely out of her mouth when she saw it to her right, leaning precariously against a branch. "You sure that'll hold me?"

The rickety ladder looked as if it wouldn't support a four-year-old.

"Yes," Charlyn barked.

Another ladder appeared, and Charlyn nabbed a basket and climbed into the leaves. Talia did the same and balanced the basket on top of the ladder. They worked quietly for a while until Talia's basket was full. She tried to lift it, but it was impossibly heavy.

"How am I supposed to get it down?" Talia asked.

Charlyn wrinkled her nose and pointed a finger at the apples, and they floated gently down. Then she snapped, and another empty basket appeared at the top

WHEN THE FOREST CRIES

of the ladder. Talia barely caught it before it fell to the ground.

Over the next few hours, they cleared away apples from the tree. Charlyn was floating her basket down when Zella suddenly appeared, her long orange dress rippling in the breeze.

The basket landed with a thump.

"What in tarnation is wrong with you?" Zella screamed. She ran up and began inspecting the apples. "They're bruised. What have you done?" Zella waved her hand, and Charlyn flew through the air. Her body smashed into the ground with a thud, and she squealed out in pain.

Zella stalked over and towered over her. "Do you think you can be a full-fledged witch when you can't handle a simple floating spell?" Charlyn didn't answer, and Zella stamped her foot. "Well, do you?"

"No." Charlyn winced.

Zella gave her a kick in the side. "Then get up and get back on that ladder. And if I see any more inferior work like this, I'll make you the maid again. Is that what you want?" she yelled.

"No." Charlyn hung her head as she stood. She brushed the grass off her pretty purple dress, limped to the ladder, and climbed the steps.

SUZI WIELAND

"Both of you get back to work." Zella spun around and stomped away. Talia was not used to such a sharp tongue, her mother a gentle soul and her father strong but never mean. She missed them so much.

Talia stared after Zella's retreating figure. The slight bump Charlyn had caused didn't necessitate that reaction. The apples didn't shrivel as the one Talia had eaten.

"Is she always so nasty?" Talia asked.

"Did you hear what she said?" Charlyn snapped. "I don't want to be out here all day, so get to work."

They toiled in the branches for at least another hour, and Talia's arms grew heavy, but they still had about a quarter of the apples left to pick. She heard the chatter of voices and turned towards the noise.

A group of guards advanced down the path, led by Tatum.

"Tatum," Talia yelled. He was here to rescue her. She scrambled off the ladder and froze. Zella marched towards them like an irate badger. Talia had to get there first.

"I'm right here. I'm right here." Talia ran as fast as she could, but they hadn't noticed her yet. "Tatum," she tried again and flung her arms out to grab onto him. She could go home.

WHEN THE FOREST CRIES

Talia passed right through Tatum's body, and she stumbled to the ground, rolling to a stop.

Zella stood in front of the guards, now with a smile on her face. She glanced at Talia, and her smirk grew. "What can I help you with today, kind sirs?"

Talia rolled over and sat on her behind. She blinked. Tatum and the other guards appeared wavy, as if they weren't really there, although Zella's figure remained solid.

Talia blinked again. Zella was no longer wearing the orange dress she'd once sported and was now in a brown worn dress of a poor woman.

And behind Zella, the lofty brick home and tower were also gone, replaced by a ramshackle house.

"They can't see you," Charlyn said.

This was impossible. A house could not disappear. But Zella was a witch, and Talia had no idea the extent of her powers.

"We are searching for a young lady. Princess Talia disappeared yesterday, and she was headed in this direction when last seen."

"I'm so sorry." Zella shook her head sadly. "I have seen no girls around here, but you're welcome to search my property in case she is hiding somewhere."

"That would be mighty fine of you, ma'am," Tatum said. "Miss Talia is partial to sneaking off on her own sometimes, so she may have found a hideout to stay in."

"But I'm here." Talia hopped to her feet and rushed to Tatum again. She waved her hand through his body, nothing but air. She swung for one of the guards but didn't hit anything solid. "Please don't leave me."

"Children don't always think," Zella said, hiding her grin. "I must return to my house as I have bread in the oven, but please feel free to search around." Zella stared right at Talia as she fought her tears. "I hope you find her. I'm sure her parents must miss her."

Tatum thanked Zella and ordered the crew to spread out. Zella started back to the house, and Talia rocked back and forth on her heels.

She'd never escape. She'd have to spend three long years being Zella's slave. Would Zella even release her after that? What if she accidentally bruised more apples before then?

Tears filled her eyes. Her parents—she wanted to see them so badly. She didn't know how she'd make it through the next three years with this ache in her heart.

Charlyn stared after Zella's retreating figure. "I suggest you get back to work because Zella won't be too happy with you once we return to the house."

"But why? I didn't do anything." Why would Zella blame her for Tatum and the guards stopping by?

WHEN THE FOREST CRIES

"Because," Charlyn huffed, "she was in the tower working, and you interrupted. She does not appreciate being interrupted."

Talia didn't want to finish the apple-picking because that meant she had to go back and face an angry Zella, but if they worked too slowly, Zella would be upset too.

She climbed the ladder and began the harvest once again.

Chapter Five

Back at the house, Zella lay on the sofa, her arm over her forehead, and the skirt of her orange dress hanging to the floor.

She jumped to her feet and pointed a bony finger at Talia, her face white. "How dare you bring that kind of scrutiny to my home."

She stomped over and struck Talia on the cheek. Talia stumbled back, her skin stinging. Zella took a few deep breaths, her hand at her throat as if she couldn't breathe well. "You'd better hope that doesn't happen again. Now get me a drink, you nasty girl."

Charlyn gave Talia an I-told-you-so look.

"What would you like?" If only Talia had poison to put in the drink.

"Wine. What else would I want?" Zella stalked to the sofa and sunk down, huffing for air. Then she stared at Charlyn. "Well, help her. Do you think she can get it herself? What's wrong with you?"

WHEN THE FOREST CRIES

Charlyn trudged out of the room and down a small hall. At the end was an imposing doorway that creaked as she opened it.

Talia followed her through and gazed at the grand site in front of her. A metal staircase rose in the middle of a round room, each step a black stone that sparkled with flecks of gold.

The doorway hit Talia in the behind, and she jumped forward, letting it shut. Charlyn gave her an irritated look and waved for her to follow.

She was unable to see the top of the stairs no matter how much she craned her neck.

"Let's go," Charlyn snapped, already three steps up.

Talia rushed to catch up and gripped the cool metal rail, still staring up. They passed a landing with a golden Z inscribed into the black stone. The landing butted up next to a wall, and a flaming sconce lit the surrounding area, but no door was apparent.

Another floor up was the same thing. Talia ran her fingers over the smooth wall but felt nothing. It had to be some kind of trick, magic hiding them. There would be no other reason for a landing.

Six more flights they marched until, finally, Charlyn stopped. She drew a Z on the wall with her finger, and a door materialized. She seized the knob and pushed

30

SUZI WIELAND

into the room. Talia gaped at the floor-to-ceiling racks of wine bottles. She slowly roamed around and then back to the door, studying the hundreds and hundreds of bottles. Perhaps thousands.

She pulled out a bottle and stared at the front. A big Z was etched into the green glass.

"Don't mix them up," Charlyn sniped.

"I only took one out." She ran her thumb over the Z. "Does she make her own wine?" Was this what she was doing with those apples they'd harvested? She couldn't believe Zella had enslaved her for three years over an apple to make wine.

One gosh darn apple.

Charlyn held two bottles in her hands. "Yes, Zella does many things. Her wine is quite popular. Now put it back." Charlyn took the bottles in one hand and planted her free hand on her hip. "Zella's waiting."

She watched Talia put the bottle back, grabbed a third bottle, and handed it over, and motioned to go out. As soon as the door shut behind Charlyn, it disappeared, and the wall looked blank again.

The girls trudged downstairs and into the kitchen. Charlyn filled a glass and scuttled into the parlor. Zella sat up on the sofa, acting as if it was too much effort. She took the glass and downed it quickly.

WHEN THE FOREST CRIES

"Fill me another," Zella commanded, flopping back and holding up the empty glass. "No, just grab the bottle."

Talia followed Charlyn to the kitchen. "What's wrong with her? She looks exhausted."

"That spell took a lot out of her. It's not hard to camouflage the house from people passing by, but there were a group of men on the property today. It taxed her greatly."

Serves her right.

"Where's my wine?" Zella screeched, and Talia picked a bottle and returned to the other room. Zella snatched it out of Talia's hand. "Now get out of my sight. I don't want to see you anymore."

Talia got some food from the kitchen and ate, then tiptoed up the stairs. The bedroom was empty, and she retreated to the window to stare at the grounds bathed in the dying light.

The tower lay off to the side, but she still couldn't see the top. Maybe she could get in there and find out a way to escape—a magical escape. Maybe she had to go up to get out. But who knew? It was worth a try.

She yawned, her arms and back aching from the work today. She had a newfound respect for those who kept the castle running every day.

SUZI WIELAND

I will make it back home, she promised herself. There had to be a chance to find an escape.

After washing up, she slipped into bed. Charlyn still hadn't returned after a few hours, and she fell asleep in the empty room.

Chapter Six

Zella sniped at Talia all during breakfast. The food was too hot. The food was too cold. The food was tasteless.

Which was ridiculous because Zella had magicked everything to her liking.

Talia was soon left alone after Zella and Charlyn disappeared into the tower. She had her list of jobs though and worried that she might not finish by lunch as Zella insisted.

But lunch came and went, and then dinner. Talia's back throbbed from all the bending over, but she had more chores to do. Soon, it was past eight.

She swept the floor, humming a tune her mother used to sing when they were picking up toys. Mother had the most beautiful voice she'd ever heard, but Talia only hummed because her voice was not of the same caliber. The song made her heart ache, but at the same time, gave her comfort. She would see her mother again.

In three years.

"Well, what do we have here?" a deep voice said. Talia spun around and came face-to-face with a devastatingly handsome young man with thick brown hair and wide gray eyes. He smiled at her. "And who are you?"

Talia set the broom aside and straightened. This man might help her get away, show her how to get through the invisible tree-wall.

"My name's Talia." She gave him a curtsey.

"Mother didn't say she was accepting another apprentice. She is so generous, wanting to lift up the poor and downtrodden." His head tilted to the side, and he gave her an enormous smile.

Talia held back her scream. Of course this was Zella's son—except for his curly brown hair, he looked just like her. All thoughts for escape disappeared into thin air.

"I'm… I'm…" Her mind was fuzzy from the way he was looking at her.

The man raised his hand and ran it through Talia's long blonde hair. "Silky and stunning. What do you use on your golden locks?" He let the strands fall.

Talia stepped back. The nerve of this man.

"Bishop!" Zella burst through the door, running for her son with arms open wide. He hauled her in for a

WHEN THE FOREST CRIES

hug as Charlyn shuffled into the room, a smile brightening her face.

"You're a day early," Zella gushed. "What are you doing home already?" She released her son and stood back to study him. "You look thinner. Have you been eating properly? You must be working too hard."

"I'm fine, Mother." He rolled his eyes. "I had everything done, so I decided to come home. But who is this sweet gal over here?" He gave Talia the most charming look, and the smiles fell away from both Zella's and Charlyn's faces.

"She is a thief. She will be working off her debt over the next three years." Zella's scowl deepened as she stared at Talia. She retreated to the sofa and sat, smoothing out the yellow skirt of her velvet dress.

"Interesting." He rubbed his chin as he eyed Talia, but then his eyes flicked to Charlyn. "Hello, Charlyn. Nice to see you again," he said in a much cooler voice.

"The same to you." She nodded and stepped to arrange some books on the bookshelf.

"Thief, get us some wine. We must celebrate my son's return from the university." Zella linked her arm in Bishop's and led him to the sofa.

"How many glasses should I get?" Talia asked, glancing at Charlyn.

SUZI WIELAND

"Two of course, you fool," Zella snarled, but then smiled for her son. "I'm glad to have you home. I've missed you."

Charlyn slunk off, and Talia returned to the kitchen to get the wine. After Talia served the two, Zella finally released her, and she stepped outside for some fresh air.

She stared at the apple trees, wondering why they were so important. Maybe Zella sold the apples at the market for an exorbitant price in addition to making the wine.

Talia wandered to the front of the property. A wagon rumbled by, a man and woman. She called out, but of course, nobody heard her, the invisibility still there. She sat down and hugged her legs, thinking of her parents and how heartbroken they must be. They would know she'd never leave them by choice, so they probably assumed her dead by now.

Something soft touched her shoulder, and she jumped, but it was just the leaves from the tree next to her blowing in the breeze. She raised her arm and ran her hand over the rough grayish-brown bark. It felt moist, as if there'd been a rain recently, but the skies were clear and bright.

She'd never sit in the backyard swing under the shade, listening to her mother tell stories of the old

WHEN THE FOREST CRIES

days. She'd never again play a game of croquet with her father. He didn't let her win anymore, but he used to when she was young.

There were so many things she'd never again do.

At twilight, she returned to her room, grateful for the sleep that would soon come. Mother and son were still drinking downstairs, fiddle music playing loudly, but the walls buffered the noise.

Not long after Talia retired to bed, she heard Charlyn slip into the room and onto her bed. Talia pretended to be asleep and didn't open her eyes until Charlyn had lain down.

Talia couldn't yet tell if Charlyn was friend or foe. Charlyn often snapped at her, but if she befriended the girl, perhaps Charlyn would help her escape.

Some noises in jolted Talia awake. Hushed whispers and a giggle. "Be quiet, Bishop." Charlyn laughed.

"We don't need to be quiet. Mother's out cold downstairs. She'll never hear us."

"Maybe, but you'll wake her." The word *her* contained much venom, and Talia guessed Charlyn was pointing at her.

"Then she can watch." Bishop sat atop Charlyn and spread her hair over her shoulders. Then he leaned down.

SUZI WIELAND

The sounds of kissing replaced the words, and soft moans filled the room as the bed started rocking. Talia could picture a naked Bishop on top of Charlyn, and she squeezed her eyes shut. The grunting and heavy breaths got louder and louder, and Talia covered her ears, not caring if they knew she was awake, but neither of them noticed.

Good golly, he had his own room. Why couldn't they be in there?

Bishop collapsed next to Charlyn.

"Did you miss me while you were gone?" Charlyn asked.

"More than anything."

"Did you break up with that Josephine girl?"

"Of course, sweetums. You're the only one for me." They grew quiet, and Charlyn let out a giggle.

"I'd better return to my bed. I don't want to fall asleep and have Mother find us in the morning. I'd rather stay with you though. One day we'll be together."

Bishop climbed out of bed and stared towards Talia, fully exposed. She smashed her eyes closed, and he said a quiet goodnight to Charlyn and strode out of the room, clothes in hand.

Charlyn sighed in contentment and snuggled into her blankets. Talia finally got some peace.

Chapter Seven

Talia prepared lunch while Zella and Charlyn worked in the tower. She hadn't yet seen Bishop this morning.

But speak of the sly fox. His mother had no idea about the clandestine affair he was having with Charlyn.

Bishop strode into the kitchen and stood next to her by the counter. Close—very close—their hips almost touching.

"Did you enjoy the show last night?" he asked, a lewd smirk on his face. He leaned in to her, nudged her hair back with his nose, and took a deep breath.

Talia's face burned hotter than the stove, and she shoved him away. "What show?"

"Hee hee. You did then." He placed his hand on her shoulder, and Talia cringed. "The Bishop train is always open for business. Day or night. The ladies love Bishop." He rubbed his fingers at the base of her neck as if he was giving her a massage.

"I don't think so." She shuffled away. "I'm sorry. I have lunch to prepare, and if it's not ready when your mother shows up, she will be upset." Talia rushed to the cupboard to get the plates to set the table, and thankfully, when she turned around, he was gone.

What a filthy dolt he was.

Fifteen minutes later, he returned with his mother and Charlyn, and they sat to eat.

Zella stared at Talia with narrow eyes and pursed lips. Talia wasn't sure what she had done wrong now. Finally, Zella focused her glare on Charlyn.

"Charlyn, your clothes are horrid." She waved her hand at Talia.

"I'm sorry." Charlyn sank into her seat.

Talia glanced at the dazzling green dress Zella wore, the bodice covered in intricate beadwork. Talia's dress, on the other hand, was a different story. The buttons were not evenly spaced, and the top bunched up funny. She wasn't the same size as Charlyn, and the girl had magicked a bunch of clothes for her, most of them having something wrong with them. Funny coloring or uneven hems, a sleeve that was longer than the other. Talia had thought it had been on purpose, to punish her for something.

"I think it's fine, Mother," Bishop chided. "It won't be long until you're able to sell Charlyn's clothes in the stores too."

WHEN THE FOREST CRIES

"You have a store in town?" Talia wracked her brain, trying to think of which it could be.

"No," Zella snapped. "We can't sell our wares around here. They would question where they came from. I'm a humble woman in a small shack. I have no means to produce such clothing." Zella slid her plate away and rubbed her temples.

"Are you okay, Mother?" Bishop set down his fork and peered across the table at her.

"Just a headache. They're coming on more often now since *she* arrived."

"Then let me go," Talia sputtered. It was so easy.

"You stole from me, thief," Zella growled. Talia flung back against her chair, an unseen force squeezing her throat.

She. Couldn't. Breathe.

Talia clawed at her neck, trying to get more air. She would die, right here in this house.

"I think she gets the point," Bishop said with a laugh. "My mother doesn't tolerate insolence," he added.

The pressure around Talia's neck released, and she gasped for air as Charlyn smirked.

That girl was definitely her foe.

"I'm starting to think that the thief has too much time on her hands. Idleness corrupts the mind, after

42

SUZI WIELAND

all." Zella stared at Talia for a few moments. "You can take over some more of Charlyn's duties so she has more time to concentrate on her work."

Talia shrunk inside but kept the emotion off her face. She had so much to do and wasn't sure how she'd get all those chores done in the day.

Thank the heavens their plates were soon emptied, and they left the room for Talia to do the dishes. She'd rather be alone than be with any of these unstable people.

Her shoulders curled forward, and she set her trembling hands onto the counter. She might not have died today, but she had three more years to get through, and someday Zella's anger would flare when Bishop wasn't here to tell her enough. Nobody would know what happened to her.

Not her friends. Not her family. Mother and Father would spend their whole lives wondering where she'd gone, and they'd die heartbroken.

She wiped the tears sliding down her cheek and stared out the windows into the trees. Their branches drooped in the hot afternoon sun, and an overwhelming sadness gripped her.

She would never be free.

Chapter Eight

One week in captivity had passed.

Seven days of hard labor with multiple indecent proposals from Bishop. He had to be crazy to think she'd have relations with him. Zella would kill her. And Talia was sure the same fate would befall Charlyn if Zella found out.

Well, maybe not since they were risking her wrath. Charlyn and Bishop's mostly quiet indifference to each other kept Zella off track, but he'd been in Talia's shared room last night, for the third time since he arrived home.

"Why don't you meet in his room?" Talia couldn't help grouching to Charlyn that morning. The two had kept her awake for almost an hour.

"His room is next to hers." She said it so nonchalantly, as if she wasn't worried Talia would tell on her.

SUZI WIELAND

"So why can't she know?" Talia wanted them out of her room. Her days were long, and her body needed sleep. Every minute of it.

"Don't be a simpleton. Nobody is good enough for her dear Bishop. Certainly not me. Once I finish my apprenticeship, we'll announce our relationship, but until then, we must keep it hidden." She sighed, staring out the window. Maybe she was in love with him, but the same couldn't be said for him.

Downstairs at breakfast, Zella stood at the head of the table in her fancy blue dress and cleared her throat. "Bishop and I are running into town for errands. I trust that you two will complete your duties before I return."

She was leaving them alone. A part of Talia wanted to hope that Zella being gone would open up some route for escape, but deep inside, she knew it wouldn't be true. Zella wouldn't leave her alone unless she knew Talia couldn't run.

Talia checked her duty list: light cleaning in the morning and tending to the garden in the afternoon. She looked forward to crawling around in the dirt, even if it was only to pick weeds.

When Zella and Bishop left, Talia snuck out after them, jumping behind tree after tree to hide. Before they reached the front gravel road, their fine clothes transformed into peasant stock, and they passed

WHEN THE FOREST CRIES

through the invisible wall and strolled off down the road.

Talia tried one last time to follow them, but the wall imprisoned her, and she trudged to the house.

Charlyn glared at her from the doorway to the tower. "You need to leave Bishop alone. He's mine."

She should tell Charlyn how he'd offered to take her to the woodshed for fun, but Charlyn hadn't treated her very well, and Talia didn't feel as if she owed the girl.

"I have no interest in Bishop."

"Sure." Charlyn scoffed. "He's intelligent and handsome and powerful. I know how girls like you work. You'd better not tempt him, or I will tell Zella."

Charlyn was delusional. Maybe it would be better to tell a small lie.

"You need not worry. I have a man at home who has been courting me." Talia wished the statement were true, that a knight in shining armor would rescue her from this nightmare, but those tales never came true in real life.

"Well, he will be gone by the time you get home. He won't wait around for you." Charlyn's nose wrinkled up.

Talia threw her hands in the air. Charlyn had an answer for everything, and there was no point in arguing with the fool.

Charlyn stomped into the house and to Zella's office door. She retrieved an incredibly large book and left the door open behind her.

"What's that?" Talia asked.

"It's my spell book. I'm going to work in the tower." Charlyn crossed the room and disappeared.

A similar book still lay on the desk. Talia crept to the door, but as soon as she tried to step through, her foot hit another invisible wall.

Foiled again by Zella's magic.

Talia knelt in the dirt, removing the weeds. Voices wafted out from the back of the house. Zella, Bishop, and a girl about Talia's age rounded the corner. She was dressed slightly better than the pair, a merchant's daughter perhaps, but Talia didn't recognize her. The girl had stunning brown hair that hung to the lower part of her back.

WHEN THE FOREST CRIES

"Thank you, my dear, for helping an old woman." Zella patted the girl's arm and retreated into the house, leaving her son and the girl with sacks in their hands.

"This way," Bishop said, leading her down the path to the shed.

Talia got back to work, and within half an hour, finished. She deposited the weeds into the fire pit and gathered her tools to put away in the woodshed.

She rounded the corner and almost dropped her tools. The girl was bent over a barrel, her long hair hanging to the ground as Bishop shagged her from behind, his hands gripping her honey hair. The barrel rocked back and forth, the girl with her eyes shut.

Bishop pulled away and stood before Talia in all his glory. He motioned to himself as if to say: look at what you're missing. He had planned this, she was sure of it, and he'd wanted her to walk in on them. What a swine.

Talia turned around in disgust and stomped away. She would never want a man like Bishop to touch her. She should tell Charlyn what she witnessed.

But no.

Charlyn would accuse her of lying, of wanting to steal Bishop away for herself or some other silly fantasy.

No, Talia needed Charlyn on her side. Charlyn would have to discover the truth on her own.

Talia retreated to the kitchen to prepare some food and watched out the window as Bishop escorted the girl to the front yard.

"Zella wants to know if dinner is ready yet." Charlyn popped into the room. Talia glanced outside, but the pair was out of sight.

"Tell her five minutes."

Ten minutes later, Charlyn returned with Zella. Bishop came inside, and Charlyn's face lit up, but she quickly tempered her enthusiasm before Zella looked her way.

"Did you give the girl the proper seeds?" Zella asked Bishop.

"Of course I did, Mother." His voice was sickly sweet.

Zella looked doubtful. "Okay, because I didn't see her leave."

Bishop's brow furrowed. "I don't know which way she went. I was helping Talia put her gardening tools away."

Zella gave Talia a stink-eye and sighed. "Not only a thief, but she's lazy too."

WHEN THE FOREST CRIES

Talia opened her mouth to defend herself, but no good would come with telling the truth. Zella would never believe her over Bishop.

"Don't worry, Mother. I'll run into town again tomorrow to make sure those are the seeds she needed."

"That's my boy." Zella patted Bishop's arm and took a drink of wine. When she wasn't looking, Bishop winked at Talia.

She shook her head, but then her gaze caught Charlyn's unsmiling face. Great—now Charlyn had something to be suspicious about too.

Chapter Nine

Other than a little improper wooing, Bishop mostly left Talia alone. He must've been getting his fill of relations between his rendezvous with Charlyn and whatever other girl he could find. One day it had been the milk delivery girl, another the apothecary's assistant. Bishop had no end to his corrupt nature, often telling the girl that she was the only one.

Talia finished dusting the dresser in Zella's room and moved to the dressing table. Bishop snuck in behind her and cornered her, his body pressing into hers.

"When Mother is away, the children can play," he whispered, his breath hot on her ear. She didn't have the reaction from her he surely craved though.

"But Charlyn is not." She tried to shove him away, but he ran his fingers through the strands of her blonde hair.

"You should let me braid this beautiful hair for you."

WHEN THE FOREST CRIES

Talia pulled back. "I don't think Charlyn would appreciate that."

He laughed. "She does not care. We are just having fun."

That's not what she said. Talia opened her mouth to tell the young man off but looked at the mirror and gasped.

The image reflecting back at her was not of Bishop. It was a young man of similar age, with sad brown eyes and curly black hair. His skin was as dark as Bishop's was pale.

"What's wrong?" Bishop stared into the mirror behind her. The voice was his, but not the face, and the strange eyes showed utter confusion.

Talia spun around, and once face-to-face, found the brown-haired pale Bishop that she knew. He pressed into her bosom and snaked his arms around her waist. His hardness strained against her, and her stomach turned.

She drove him back. "I hear Charlyn," she spit out and rushed from the room. Her heart pounded. Who was that reflection she'd seen in the mirror? Bishop hadn't seemed to notice it wasn't him. Maybe it was her imagination.

SUZI WIELAND

She had to get away from him, unable to face his questions or his advances, so she went to the one place she hadn't yet been by herself.

The tower.

Nobody had forbidden her to go there, but she had seen little point as Charlyn had said she'd need magic to open the doors. But Charlyn might be lying.

The door closed behind Talia with a loud click. The staircase spiraled up the tower in front of her, and she took one step on the stairs and stopped to listen.

No noise. No Charlyn. No Bishop.

She continued on, passing by the second-floor landing and the third. She continued on and on, figuring she should try opening one of those invisible doors as Charlyn had, but she kept going. Her heart raced from exertion, and she lost track of the number of floors she passed, and she was sure it'd been at least fifteen minutes.

Maybe she should go back. But she'd come so far.

She peered up and actually saw an end to the steps. It was many landings up, but she could reach it. She continued her march to the top.

The landing was similar to the others, and she sat for a few moments to gather her breath. Her legs ached, but she stood and faced the spot where a door should

WHEN THE FOREST CRIES

be. If it didn't open, she'd go down, severely disappointed with her wasted effort.

She used her finger to draw a Z, just as Charlyn had to get to the wine cellar. A door shimmered into existence, and Talia reached for the knob, amazed it had actually worked.

She stepped through the doorway and gasped. The room opened up around her, window after window after window in a circle. Talia rushed to the closest window and took in the view.

Zella's house sat below her, surrounded by trees. A road cut a swath through the sea of green and led to town. Clouds darkened the skies, but a bright rainbow arched over the town, the place where the lives of her friends and family continued on.

The castle lay just a bit farther, at the base of the mountain range. Snow covered the white peaks high up the top of the mountains while green grass grew below in the town. Her parents had taken her into the mountain several times, and she'd marveled at how it could be winter up there and summer down below. She'd give anything now for a little lecture from her father about the weather or a trip through a field of flowers with her mother.

She covered her heart with her hand, taking in the beauty stretching out in front of her. Talia had always

SUZI WIELAND

loved the forests and lakes, but she'd never seen it laid out like this before.

Stunning.

"What are you doing here?" Charlyn huffed.

"I was…" Oh fiddlesticks. She didn't have an excuse ready.

"I sent Talia to find you," Bishop said as he trounced up the last few steps. "Mother is still gone." He wiggled his brows at her, and Charlyn giggled. "We've never had relations in the loft," he said.

"Ahh, Bishop." Charlyn sighed and wrapped herself in his arms. Talia heard the sound of sloppy kisses. His excuse made no sense at all. Why would he send Talia here to find Charlyn so he could be intimate with her?

And now he'd ruined a quiet moment of beauty.

"Have you done something different to your hair?" Bishop stepped back from Charlyn and lifted her long locks off her shoulders, running his hand through it. "It's so smooth and silky. You should grow yours longer like Talia's. You would be stunning." He embraced Charlyn and kissed her again.

Talia slipped out the door to avoid what was coming next.

Chapter Ten

On the way down, Talia thought of Bishop and the mirror. It had to be her imagination. She hadn't seen another face on his body.

But it had seemed so real, the emotion inside those eyes.

She descended the stairs for at least five minutes, unable to see the bottom.

A low sigh came from behind Talia, and she almost jumped. She steadied herself on the railing and turned. Charlyn stood behind her with a small smile and the top button of her dress undone. Where had she come from? There'd been no noise on the steps.

"Isn't he wonderful?" The dreamy look softened Charlyn's face. Did the two have relations up there? It couldn't have been that long, but Talia's sense of time might be distorted in the tower.

"Yes, wonderful. He must love you." Talia turned her head so Charlyn wouldn't see the roll of her eyes.

SUZI WIELAND

"You know he has many women who chase after him at the university, but he chose me." Charlyn passed by and took the lead.

"Yes, he did. You're very lucky." Unlucky maybe. Talia started down the steps again and passed another landing. "Are there rooms at all these floors?"

"Most. A few have high ceilings, so they take up a couple floors."

"What's in them all?"

Charlyn stopped abruptly, and Talia almost bumped into her. "There are lots of different rooms, but they all involve Zella's magic. The room where she makes the magic powder, the wine-making room. The clothes room. Others."

"What does she do with all that stuff?"

Charlyn stepped to the wall and drew a Z. The door opened, and she slipped past it. "She sells everything. Her clothes are extremely popular in other areas. And of course, her wine."

Talia followed into the room. The space only held several pieces of furniture and a few other things, and Talia peeked out the window. They appeared to be about halfway up the tower, she guessed. It was strange how there were windows here, but when she stood outside looking up, she'd seen none.

WHEN THE FOREST CRIES

Charlyn sat at the dressing table and opened a drawer. She picked up a small red glass bottle and tipped it over, dumping golden powder onto her hands. She rubbed them together and then ran her hands through her hair several times.

She dropped her hair and stared into the mirror, her lips pursed. Then she tugged on the ends and frowned.

"What are you doing?" Talia finally asked.

"Once I've finished my apprenticeship, I want to open a beauty shop where I can help women. I obviously can't do magic there, but I'll create salves and other things they can put in their hair to make it thicker or shinier or longer. And so I've been working on some magic to get better at it."

Talia needed Bishop to shower more attention on Charlyn, because that certainly affected the girl's personality. She'd never been this friendly before.

"You're trying to grow your hair longer?" Talia peered into the mirror to see if Charlyn's face had changed like Bishop's. Her reflection was normal though.

"Yes, but I can't get it to work right." Charlyn's eyes popped open, and she jumped from her seat. "Here, you sit down. I've only been able to try it on myself."

SUZI WIELAND

Before she knew it, Talia was sitting in the chair facing the mirror, and Charlyn brushed her hair. It was an odd feeling that Charlyn was being so nice, but Talia wouldn't ruin the moment.

After Charlyn brushed out Talia's braids, she poured some more powder on her hands and rubbed them together. Then she ran them through Talia's hair and said a few mumbled words that Talia couldn't understand.

Charlyn stared at her for a few moments without saying anything. Then she took more powder and did the same thing again.

Again, nothing. Talia wasn't sure if her hair was actually supposed to grow right now, but she didn't want to interrupt.

Charlyn plucked up the bottle, poured more powder on her hands, and repeated the rest of the process, ending with the words.

Talia's head tingled, and she scratched an itch. Her mouth dropped as she gazed into the mirror. Her hair was growing.

Charlyn clapped behind her and danced around. "I got it this time. I got it." She smiled from ear to ear, but Talia glanced at her reflection. Her hair had grown several inches and now hung almost down her back, and it continued to grow.

WHEN THE FOREST CRIES

This was amazing. So many women would love something to help their hair grow.

"How do you stop it?" Talia asked.

"Uh…" Charlyn stared at her with a gaping mouth.

"What do you mean, uh?" That wasn't what she wanted to hear.

Charlyn grabbed more powder, dropping the bottle to the floor. She barely rubbed her hands together before she grappled with Talia's hair.

"Ouch," Talia squealed.

New words came out of Charlyn's mouth, different from the ones she previously said. But Talia's hair kept growing.

For a few moments, Charlyn stared at Talia in horror and took off out the door, her feet pounding down the steps.

"Where are you going?" Talia screeched, running out to the landing. Her hair now stretched to the floor.

"I'll be right back," Charlyn called from several floors down.

She got the spell right but didn't know how to stop it. Would Talia's hair keep growing forever?

Talia gripped the stair railing, watching and listening for footsteps to return, but she heard nothing. Her hair slipped over the edge and hung down several floors, and it continued to lengthen.

SUZI WIELAND

How many spells had Charlyn messed up? Was this normal for apprentices? Talia wouldn't volunteer to let Charlyn experiment with her anymore.

Her hair seemed to almost reach the bottom floor, and finally, voices echoed in the stairway. Talia heard the footsteps below, but Bishop appeared right next to her. She jumped to the side, clutching her heart. He and Zella could sneak around so easily with their magic.

His smile grew as he studied her, and he peered over the railing. "This is amazing." He picked up a section of her hair and ran his fingers through it. "So soft and smooth." He held it to his nose and took a deep breath. "And smells so much like you." His eyes closed for a second, and Talia jabbed him in the side.

He laughed and started hauling the strands up and up and up. It seemed to take forever.

Eventually, he pulled the ends up and let it drop to the landing. Her hair puddled at her feet.

"Do something, please?" she begged him. She couldn't live like this, dragging a thicket of hair around all the time, cutting it constantly.

"Look at you." He stood in front of her, grasping her hair with both hands. "You're stunning with long hair."

WHEN THE FOREST CRIES

"Will you please stop it?" She'd never be able to walk this way. She wouldn't get her chores done. Zella would be furious.

Talia shook his shoulders, but he laughed. He closed his eyes and said a few words, and the growing stopped. Talia patted her head to make sure, but his words had worked.

Charlyn arrived at the landing, huffing and puffing, apparently unable to magick herself up as Bishop could. She bent over, placing her hands on her knees to prop herself up, and she sucked in mouthfuls of air.

"Please don't tell your mom." Charlyn wiped her red wet eyes.

"Why would I tell my mother? She would not appreciate what you've done here, but I can certainly appreciate your work, Charlyn." Bishop squeezed her hand, and her shoulders relaxed.

"Thank you," she said softly.

He turned to Talia. "I think we need to cut this."

The scissors magically appeared in his hand, and he reached over.

A wind seemed to rush through the stairwell, and Zella appeared. She surveyed the yards and yards of hair piled at Talia's feet, her face darkening, and she slowly pushed the sleeves of her indigo dress up. Her arms crossed, and her lips flattened.

SUZI WIELAND

Charlyn backed up a step but hit the wall.

"What did you do?" She focused her fierce gaze on Charlyn standing on the other side of the landing behind Bishop and Talia.

"I…" She gulped. "I was practicing a spell. It didn't stop growing."

Zella waved her hand in the air, and a crack rang out. Charlyn yelped and touched her cheek.

"You dim-witted twit." Zella stomped her foot like a petulant child. "I told you that you had to concentrate on other things. You have so much to learn."

"I… I'm sorry." Charlyn hung her head, still holding her cheek. "I shouldn't have done it. I should have listened to you."

"I refuse to keep you on if you continue to defy me," Zella screeched. "I'm tired of your insolence."

"Mother." Bishop stepped forward, setting himself between Zella and Charlyn. He grasped her arm and smiled. "I know Charlyn shouldn't have defied you, but it's my fault. She was practicing on Talia. I told Charlyn she needed to work on her hair. Your apprentice should be as magnificent as you are. You deserve no less."

"You encouraged her?" Zella's fury fell slightly.

"Yes, I did. She's not as pretty as you, and you and your wares deserve better. How is she to sell you products when she looks as she does?"

WHEN THE FOREST CRIES

Charlyn's lip trembled, and Talia wondered if Bishop's words hurt more than Zella's slap.

"Okay then," Zella sighed. "But I'd prefer you don't interfere with her education. She needs to learn if she is to grow."

"I apologize, Mother." Bishop dropped his head and gazed up at Zella. "I will stay out of it from now on."

"Take care of this mess." She waved to Talia's hair and disappeared as suddenly as she'd appeared.

Bishop turned to Charlyn and grasped her hands. "I'm sorry for my lies. It was the only way to weaken her anger."

Charlyn's eyes brightened. "Really?" She flung her arms around Bishop and melted into him.

"From now on, you only work on your hair around me. I will help you."

"Thank you," she murmured.

Bishop released her and stepped back, waving his hand. "Now, let's take care of this problem."

Talia's hair started moving, twisting and turning, somehow winding itself into one long braid. A hair tie appeared in his palm and then wound around her hair. He snatched the scissors from her hands and quickly cut through her thick hair.

64

SUZI WIELAND

The end of the braid thumped to the floor. Talia patted her head, glad the extra weight was gone.

She turned to thank Bishop, but he had left.

"Let's go," Charlyn sighed, heading for the steps.

"Why don't you whisk us down like they can do?" Down was better than up, but Talia just wanted to get down.

"I haven't figured it out yet," Charlyn snapped.

She should work on that rather than trying to grow people's hair. Talia kept the thought to herself though and trudged away.

Chapter Eleven

Talia couldn't stop thinking about the face in the mirror and wanted to see if it would happen again. But the next day, she was unable to get near Bishop and any of the mirrors in the house.

She was scrubbing the kitchen floor when loud voices wafted from across the room. Charlyn and Bishop must be back from their errands in town.

"What in tarnation is wrong with you?" Zella screeched.

Oh no. This wasn't good. But morbid curiosity made Talia creep towards the doorway and peer into the other room. Zella stood in front of a shrinking Charlyn, shaking a dress at her.

"Don't you recognize this, you imbecile?" Zella thrust the violet dress into her face, and Charlyn backed up, muttering a soft answer.

"What's wrong, Mother?" Bishop looked upon the two from the door, and Talia wondered how many times he saved her from his mother's outbursts.

SUZI WIELAND

"This is my dress!" Zella snapped, shoving Charlyn onto the sofa. She hurled the crumpled dress at a quivering Charlyn and turned to Bishop. "Do you remember two months ago when Richter told me about the fire in his barn?"

"Yes, so?" He glanced at Charlyn indifferently.

"This is one of the dresses he claimed was burned." The fury flared in Zella's eyes as she paced up and down in front of the sofa. "He's stolen my dresses and is selling them. He won't get away with it though. He cannot claim my work as his own." Zella pounded her fist on her palm.

"Whatever will you do?" Bishop's eyes finally held some type of emotion: interest.

Zella spun around to face Charlyn. "Well, first, we will bind your powers."

"Wait, why?" Charlyn started to stand, but Zella slapped her back into place.

"How could you not recognize my designs? You just spent money on my own dress. A lot of money. Be lucky it's only for a week."

Talia hadn't known binding powers was possible. Maybe that was her key to escaping. Zella had two spell books, one in the office and another in the tower, and if Talia could get to them, she could attempt the spell on Bishop or Charlyn before trying it on Zella. She needed

67

WHEN THE FOREST CRIES

some of that magic powder though. Bishop and Zella didn't use it for all their magic, but Charlyn required it.

"You will go to that store tomorrow," Zella directed. "And tell the woman who sold it to you that she needs to send word to the dressmaker that a wealthy client wants to purchase more. And that the dressmaker should bring the selections himself. A hefty sum will be paid. Now get out of my face," she spat.

Charlyn scrambled off the sofa.

"Go work on the harvest," Zella yelled.

"What are you going to do?" Bishop raised his brows at his mother conspiratorially.

"I'm not sure yet. I want you to take the thief to the harvest room to help Charlyn, then come back to my office. We have a lot to discuss."

Talia had to get to that binding spell, except Zella magicked the doorway to the office, and Talia couldn't get in to search for the book. She needed a way to access the spell book.

"Let's go, thief," Bishop said to Talia, as if it was a joke, and she followed him into the tower. He stopped at the bottom of the steps. "Floor twenty," he said, and before Talia even blinked, she was standing on the landing. Bishop drew a Z on the door and opened it for her.

SUZI WIELAND

"The thief is here to help you." Bishop laughed again and nudged her inside, shutting the door behind her.

A basket floated through the air, and Charlyn set it gently on the table. "Get one of the baking sheets and do this." She started removing apples from the basket and set them on the sheet. Two rows of four, spaced evenly apart.

Talia stood there for a minute or so, just watching. After Zella's lashing, Talia had thought Charlyn would retreat to the corner to cry.

Charlyn glanced up with furious eyes. "Didn't I tell you to get to work?" She crossed her arms and waited for Talia to move before turning back and muttering under her breath. "Idleness corrupts a mind."

Talia filled up a sheet with apples, thinking about Charlyn and remembering how Zella had thrown that same phrase out before. In fact, Charlyn parroted a lot of the things Zella said. The girl probably wanted to take over for Zella someday.

Talia kept placing apples while Charlyn stoked the fires in the ovens to roaring hot. Then they loaded the ovens with the sheets. Four trays in each.

"You're baking the apples?" Talia asked.

"No. It's magic powder." Charlyn rolled her eyes. "Just watch."

WHEN THE FOREST CRIES

She took a bottle from the table and dumped a teaspoon of golden powder onto her hands. Then she went to the oven and opened the door, standing off to the side. She tossed in the powder, and the flames flared up, the scorching heat reaching Talia.

"Whoa. That's hot." Talia backed up.

Charlyn closed the door and moved onto the next stove, doing the same thing.

"What is the powder you're using?" she tried again.

"Magic powder."

"And what are we doing?"

"We're making more powder," Charlyn said in an irritated voice. Talia had more questions, but she decided to stay quiet for a bit.

Charlyn repeated the process at each of the six stoves and then returned to the first. She removed a tray and brought it to a special slotted holder. Each sheet now held eight piles of golden powder.

Talia wiped her sweaty forehead. The temperatures in the stove had to be super high to create that powder in only seconds.

"Grab a tray and put it in a slot." Charlyn pointed to a second glove sitting on the counter.

After a few trays, Talia was sweating all over. She carefully removed another one and made sure Charlyn

SUZI WIELAND

was out of the way before walking away. She didn't want to burn herself or Charlyn.

By the time they moved the sheets, Charlyn took the tray on the lowest level and set it on the table. "They cool off fast," she said and took out another.

Talia couldn't believe they'd lose heat that quickly, but Charlyn wasn't using her glove, and so when Talia fingered a tray, her fingers met a warm, but not hot, surface.

The tabletop only had room for eight trays, and Talia held a bowl still while Charlyn brushed the fine, golden powder into it. Talia reached into the bowl to touch it.

Charlyn's hand shot out. "What are you doing? Zella will punish you if you waste any powder."

Talia rubbed her fingers together, a tiny bit of powder on them. "It's barely anything."

"Do you not remember what she did because you took out one of her apples?"

Talia remembered. Very clearly.

"This is the powder that allows you to do magic?"

"Yes. I have to use powder most of the time, but the more powerful a witch becomes, the less she needs to rely on it. Bishop doesn't use much of it either. Not unless it's a considerable spell. Some spells require only powder, and more complex ones require other

WHEN THE FOREST CRIES

ingredients in addition to large quantities of powder. It's in her spell book."

"What's a big spell?"

Suspicious eyes studied Talia. "Cloaking her house constantly from prying eyes. A binding." Charlyn sighed.

Talia needed to get her hands on that book, but she couldn't get into the office where Zella kept it.

"Can I do a spell? Even a little one?"

Charlyn scoffed. "No. And besides, Zella would kill me."

Which meant that if Talia could actually see a spell and get the powder, she might be able to handle a simple one.

"It's not as easy as it looks." Charlyn eyed her again.

"I'm sure it isn't."

After filling the bowls with powder, Charlyn took a special cup to scoop it out and dumped it through a funnel into a bottle. They filled bottle after bottle and repeated the whole process again.

A few hours later, Talia's damp clothes were sticking to her skin. She needed a breath of cool air. Finally, they cleaned up and put everything away. The bottles remained on the table.

"Where do we bring these?" Talia asked.

"I'll let Bishop handle this. I'm pretty sure Zella doesn't want me showing you where we store the magic powder. Let's go."

Talia sighed. Charlyn wouldn't be any help if she wanted to escape. At least she was learning more about her prison. It might make her time here go faster.

That evening, Talia finished her chores and found Zella and Bishop downstairs, no Charlyn around.

"Is there anything else you need done, Zella?" she asked.

The witch put her book down and sighed. "Yes. A glass of wine for both of us."

Bishop jumped out of his seat and followed Talia to the kitchen. "We've got time for a kiss." Bishop reached for her waist, but she shoved him away. "Don't worry. Charlyn's not around either."

"No." Talia clunked the bottle on the counter. Thank the heavens she didn't need to run and get a bottle from the tower. Bishop would probably have followed her. He thought he was endearing, but he was a clod. She poured the glasses and left his there while she delivered Zella hers.

WHEN THE FOREST CRIES

They passed by a small decorative mirror on the wall, and even though Bishop wasn't looking directly into it, Talia could see the dark skin belonging to the reflection.

"Bishop, what…" She stopped. A twinge inside her made her think she shouldn't mention the mirror thing to him.

"What, what?" he said.

"I'm waiting," Zella screeched.

Talia smiled. "I was just about to ask what type of wine you prefer. But we'd better get back to your mother."

She scuttled off to Zella, not wanting to get yelled at again.

Chapter Twelve

Every day for the last week, Talia tried to get another glimpse of the mystery reflection, but other than a quick side glance into the mirror, she didn't get to see much.

She almost needed Bishop to approach her as he had in his mother's room that one day, but 1.) she didn't want to be trapped by him again. And 2.) it rarely happened that they were caught alone together.

Talia watered the plants in the garden after another weeding.

"Zella wants you to come out front for the show," Charlyn said from the corner of the house. The girl had whined and moaned this last week because she had no powers, and Talia would be happy when she got them back.

Talia came around, and Charlyn waved her over. Down the path through the trees, a man made his way with a wagon full of wares.

WHEN THE FOREST CRIES

The clothing. Talia had almost forgotten. A silent dread filled her as she remembered Zella's reaction to what the man had done.

"This should be interesting," Charlyn whispered.

But not for the man. Talia held back her comment.

His wagon pulled to a stop, and he climbed down, a child about ten in his wake.

"Hello. I'm looking for the madam of the house," the man said with a polite nod, but his brow furrowed. Talia turned back and gasped. The house was now a small cottage, the one she'd seen the first day. This was not the home of a woman about to buy expensive dresses.

Zella swept out the door in the infamous violet dress, Bishop trailing behind, and the man bowed his head. "Good morning, madam." He eyed her clothing and the house. "My name is—"

"Richter. Yes, I'm aware." Zella smiled darkly, and the man glanced at his young son. "I just love this dress, don't I, Bishop?" Zella continued.

"Yes, you do." He smiled as gleefully as her. His skin darkened, and his face changed into the one Talia had seen in the mirror.

She blinked, but his face returned to normal. It had to have been her imagination.

"Did you see that?" she said to Charlyn.

76

"See what?" Charlyn glowered at her, and Talia shut up. Bishop looked their way, and for a moment, she was staring at someone different. She could've sworn he mouthed the words, "Help me."

She shook her head, but the vision was gone, replaced with the normal Bishop. Zella hadn't seemed to notice what was going on either.

"This is my son, Bishop, and I presume that little boy is your own?" Zella waved at the boy standing next to his father, her voice light.

"Yes, my firstborn. I'm teaching him the ways of a merchant."

"And are you teaching him to cheat others?" she said politely.

Richter did a double take and stared at Zella, his mouth agape. "Of course not."

"So who is the seamstress who made this dress?" Zella grinned slyly and studied the sleeve of her dress. "I must have her name."

"My wife," Richter said proudly. "She is a wonderful seamstress, as you can see."

Zella stepped over to the child and ruffled his hair. "What a sweet boy. This is your wife's handiwork? She's awfully talented. May I see some others?"

WHEN THE FOREST CRIES

"Surely you can." Richter wandered around the back of the wagon, and Talia watched Zella watching the boy with a steady gaze. Talia's hackles rose.

Richter brought around four dresses and hung them along the side of the wagon, careful to make sure they did not touch the ground.

"Are those hers?" Talia whispered to Charlyn. The dresses were every bit as gorgeous as the ones Zella wore.

"Three of them. I'm pretty sure the fourth isn't."

"Why doesn't he recognize her? Didn't he buy a bunch of dresses from her?" Talia was trying to figure this all out.

"She's changed her looks. We just can't see what she looks like. Now shush."

Zella fingered the fabric on the first dress. "These are exquisite. Your wife again?"

"Yes, yes." He nodded and brought around two more dresses. "This is my stock. Are there any you wish to try on?"

"That's not necessary. I'll take these four." Zella piled the dresses in her arms and handed them off to Bishop.

"All four?" Richter said, a gleam growing in his eyes.

78

SUZI WIELAND

"Yes, but I won't be paying for them." Zella tilted her head to the side. The sweet grin on her face hid the anger about to explode. She'd ranted and raved this whole week about the man who had stolen her dresses and claimed them as his own.

Talia clenched her hands together, not wanting to look, not wanting to call any attention to herself.

"I'm afraid I don't understand. My wife put a lot of work into those dresses."

Zella raised her hand and snapped. Talia didn't know what Richter had been seeing, but now his eyes were opened. He backed away from the witch.

"Zella. I… I, um…"

"No words now? You don't want to tell me how your wife slaved over these clothes?" Zella spit out, shaking her finger at him. "Or about the fire that destroyed *my* hard work. The hard work that I was benevolent enough not to charge you for even though it was your shed that burned? The hard work that you are now claiming as your own?"

"I didn't know how to find you. I thought they burned, but they didn't," he stammered, his hands in his pockets.

Zella clucked her tongue and shook her head. "No, there was no fire. I checked. Just a greedy man and woman and their tree."

WHEN THE FOREST CRIES

"Our tree?" Richter said after a pause.

Zella waved her hand and sent a handful of powder flying into the air as she mumbled some words. Richter's son disappeared, replaced by a tall leafy tree. Richter gasped and ran to the trunk as a heaviness descended on the scene, and a mournful breeze seemed to pass through the leaves.

"No, no, no!" he howled. "Terrence, no." Richter wrapped his arms around the tree and dropped to his knees, tears wetting the rough bark. "Please, Zella. He's done nothing wrong. He's only a child."

Talia couldn't breathe, couldn't think. This was an innocent boy.

"I'll do anything," he begged, his red cheeks wet. "I'll give you anything. You can take me. Please give me my son back."

Zella flipped her hand over, palm up, and raised her arm. Richter awkwardly got to his feet, his eyes wide as he looked at his legs.

"I'll give you two choices." Zella's head tilted to the side, and she glanced at the tree before focusing on Richter again. "You can either leave this beautiful tree here for me to enjoy for the rest of my years, or we can chop it down right now, and you can bring the firewood home to your wife."

SUZI WIELAND

"No." Richter paled. "Don't chop him down. Please, no."

"Then be on your way." Zella snatched the four dresses and stalked towards the house.

Richter stared blankly at the tree, tears flooding his face. He touched the bark tenderly, his lip trembling. He stood there until Zella cleared her throat.

Then he trudged to his wagon. He sat for a few moments, reins in hand, despair on his face, and with a sob, he led the horses down the path to the road.

Zella strode for the door, with Charlyn and Bishop following. This was wrong. So, so wrong. Her heart broke for the boy. Was he dead? Did he see what was going on?

A droplet of water hit her hand, and she peered up into the wilting branches above her. Trees were not living creatures and did not show emotion, but this one sure seemed to look how she felt.

Maybe her three years of working off her debt wasn't the worst thing in the world.

Chapter Thirteen

Talia lay in bed, the events of the day running through her mind. Yes, she was even more afraid of Zella, but her resolve also strengthened. Zella's powers needed binding. She was an evil woman who must be stopped, and Talia needed to be careful as she tried to discover how to find the binding spell.

The man in the mirror was the other mystery too.

Wait—a mirror.

Talia stared at Charlyn's sleeping figure. Bishop must be in his room too. She could bring a small mirror to him and test his reflection. It might be too dark, but if he slept with his windows open too, then maybe she could see the image again.

Quietly, she snuck out of bed, found her slippers, and crept down the hall to the washroom to find a mirror. His door was closed, and she opened it slowly to avoid any squeaking of hinges. If he woke up, he'd get the wrong idea, and she didn't want to have to fight him.

SUZI WIELAND

Bishop lay under his covers, only his head showing. She shut his door in case Zella woke up and tiptoed to his bed. Talia held the mirror above his face, and sure enough, the other man's image reflected back, eyes closed like Bishop.

"Who are you?" Talia whispered.

The eyes flew open, and Talia jumped backwards. The mirror clattered to the floor, and she dropped to her knees and held her breath. She counted to a hundred, but Bishop didn't stir, so she picked up the mirror and stood, holding it over his head again.

The face seemed as confused as she was.

"Talia?" a quiet voice said, and she startled again, but this time grasped the handle tightly. The voice belonged to Bishop but was softer and gentler.

"What's your name?" she asked.

"Xavier. Can you really see me?"

She nodded. "I can't believe I'm talking to a mirror. How is this possible?"

"It happened when both Bishop and I were six, although I didn't know him. He contracted a disease and was dying. Zella took his soul and put it in my body but then spelled me so it looked like him. I have no control over anything he does or says, but I'm here."

WHEN THE FOREST CRIES

"You're stuck in his head… all the time?" So Xavier was a witness to the debauchery Bishop participated in. Poor man.

She shook her head. That would be the least of his worries. He'd essentially lost his life.

"I am. I think she messed up when she did it, and I was supposed to die. How did you see me? Nobody's ever seen me before."

"I don't know. It was just in the mirror. And then today I saw you when Richter was here."

"Yes, the boy…" Xavier's face darkened, his eyes sad. "Will you help me get out?"

Talia didn't answer right away. She had no idea if Xavier was being truthful. He could be a rogue himself.

"Where are you from?" she asked.

"Larvik."

"Okay." She'd heard of Larvik, but it was a few days' travel by train. Her father had probably been there before though.

"How did you end up here? I mean, I know how, but why didn't your parents find you?"

"Because she kidnapped me and brought me here. Sixteen years ago."

Sixteen years. Talia was lamenting her three years of captivity when Xavier had been imprisoned for so much longer. And yet, he felt sorrow for Richter's son.

SUZI WIELAND

Xavier was a decent man. She knew it deep inside her heart.

"Of course I'll help you. What do we need to do?"

"You have to kill me," he said with utmost sincerity. Talia almost laughed, but Xavier didn't let loose a smile.

"But if I kill you, you're dead." And Bishop would be dead. And she would be a murderer.

"I won't really die, as long as you say the spell properly. Bishop's life will end, and mine will take over again."

"Does he know you're inside him?"

"No. It's not as if I can talk to him or anything, and he and the others are blind to my reflection. They only see what they want to see, which is Bishop. Not even Charlyn knows."

"What am I supposed to kill you with?" She looked around the room for a weapon, but he chuckled.

"We can't do it now. This will take some planning. I've memorized the spell over the years as I've seen Bishop study the spell book. It's not an easy spell, and I'm sure it'll take you days to learn it and say it properly."

"Wait, does that mean you know the binding spell?" Right after he escaped, they could bind Zella and Charlyn.

WHEN THE FOREST CRIES

"No. I only memorized the one I needed. But I can search for others if he's looking at the book."

That could take so long. Bishop knew a lot now and probably knew the binding spell.

"I haven't seen him look at the spell book once since I've gotten here. I'm not sure how or why he'd do it now."

"I don't know. We'll figure it out. Why don't we think about it a bit and come back and talk in a few days. Maybe one of us will have an idea."

"Okay," she said sadly. This wouldn't work, and she couldn't risk killing Bishop until she had that binding spell. Otherwise Zella or Charlyn would kill her.

"Hey, we'll be okay. We'll both get out of here and get home to see our families again. I have hope."

He sounded confident, but Talia could only think about the boy from earlier who now was a part of Zella's yard. She didn't want to become a tree.

Chapter Fourteen

Two nights passed, and Talia wasn't able to slip back to Bishop's room, but she thought often of the unfortunate man and how he spent his life.

Did he feel the warm water of a nice bath? Did he taste the food Bishop ate? Did he experience the emotions Bishop felt?

She had so many questions for him.

On the afternoon of day three, Zella and Charlyn were locked away in the tower, and Talia figured she might as well try get information from Bishop.

She knocked on the office door, and Bishop opened it up.

"Come to see me?" He grinned.

"Not for that." She sighed. "I had some questions about the spell book." Talia had tried to ask Charlyn about spellings and magicking, but she never shared anything.

"Come in. What did you want to know?"

WHEN THE FOREST CRIES

"I can't." She reached out and felt the invisible wall between them.

"I forgot." Bishop flicked his wrist, and Talia's hand fell forward through the open space. She strode into the room, her heart pounding. Would he really allow her to see the spell book? This was too easy.

Talia took a seat in the extra chair and dragged it up to the book.

"What do you want to know?" he asked again.

She touched the book tentatively, but he didn't say to keep away.

"How does it work? Are there ingredients for all spells, or do you just say the words?" She opened the book and frowned. Then she flipped another page and another, her stomach clenching. It was gibberish. Nothing made sense.

"They're all different. Some easier spells don't require ingredients or powder, but tougher ones do. Experienced witches have used so much powder that it is absorbed into our skin, so we don't always need it. Except for the more difficult spells."

His explanation was similar to Charlyn's at least.

"Um, what about the binding spell? That must be a hard one since Charlyn can't use her powers." Thank the heavens Zella had done that, and now it wouldn't seem odd that Talia was asking about it. She hoped he'd

SUZI WIELAND

flip to that page, even though she couldn't read it. Xavier could.

Bishop folded his hands and placed them behind his head, watching her. "Yup. That one's more difficult."

"Could you teach me how to do a spell?" She gave him her most captivating smile.

He laughed. "No. Mother won't allow it."

Oh, now he chose to listen to his mother?

He slammed the book shut. "But…" The office door closed behind them. "I could cast a spell so you find me irresistible."

He wouldn't, would he?

She realized right then that he could've magicked her at any point. He could've taken her without her permission. The room suddenly felt hot.

"Relax." He chuckled. "I don't force women to want me. What fun is that then?" He leaned into his chair, hands behind his head again. "Besides, Mother's got a thing about people and free will."

Talia scoffed. "The woman who turned a child into a tree? The woman imprisoning me for three years for taking a bite from an apple?"

That was the most ridiculous thing she'd heard.

"It was a magic apple." He shrugged. "One apple contains an extreme amount of magic. And Richter

WHEN THE FOREST CRIES

tried to cheat her. Mother does not like to be taken advantage of."

"But she's got hundreds of trees. How much magic does she need?"

Bishop's gaze dropped to Talia's chest. "Let me tell you a story. But you have to close your eyes."

Talia did as directed. Yes, he was a clod, but he must've been truthful about what he'd said about not taking women by force. He would've done it by now.

"Once upon a time," he started, "there were three people who lived in a house. Two exquisite ladies and a handsome, charming fellow. The spicy dames often enticed the fellow by baring their massive bosoms and delighted in—"

"Bishop." She sighed.

"Okay, okay. Sorry." His chair scraped the floor, and he continued. "The two girls shared a room at night, Teeny and Tiny. One night, they were bored, and Teeny crawled into bed with Tiny, both completely naked."

"I'm done." She opened her eyes and stood, her mouth dropping. Bishop sat in the chair with his hand in his pants.

"Wait. I'm not done. The girls totally—"

Talia stormed out and slammed the door behind her. She was so ready to get out of this place.

90

Chapter Fifteen

That night, after everyone was asleep, Talia crept down the hall to Bishop's room again. She held the mirror over his face. Xavier opened his eyes but avoided her gaze.

"I'm sorry for, um…" he started.

For Bishop. It wasn't as if Xavier could do anything about it.

"Don't worry about it. He's a cad."

"And then some." Xavier sighed. "I'm so tired of the way he uses these women. The lies he tells to get them in bed."

It wasn't just Bishop's bad deeds, but he'd probably witnessed Zella's evil over and over again.

"What happens after we kill his soul?" she whispered. "How will we get away from Zella?"

"That's the problem. I don't know if the illusion of Bishop will disappear, if Zella and Charlyn will see him, or if they'll see me. If they see him, we'll be home free, but if not…"

WHEN THE FOREST CRIES

"Then we need another plan. We can't risk it. Her power is too strong."

"I've been thinking about that. We should wait for a day when Zella goes into town, and you need to get him outside, somewhere Zella wouldn't go. You recite the spell and then stab him... Me."

"What if something goes wrong?" A thousand things could happen.

"It's a risk I must take." He finally gazed into her eyes. "I can get you out of the wall and away from her."

But what if he couldn't? And Zella would not give her up so easily. She would eventually search for them. Talia would never know if the person she was speaking to was actually Zella, about to kidnap her again.

"But we need to bind her powers. I'm sure I can get Bishop to open the page to the binding spell so you can read it. I was unable today though."

"Perhaps." Xavier nodded.

Another thought struck Talia. "What if I somehow get Charlyn in trouble? Zella would probably bind her for a week. During that week, we bind Zella. She won't let me go."

"No, she won't." Xavier sighed, his face somber. "Talia, do you understand that you have to kill people? In order for me to live, we have to take out Bishop. And I'm pretty sure that for us to escape, we need to kill Zella. Even if a binding spell works, it'd only be temporary. She will figure out how to undo it. But we can kill her if you take her by surprise. She's not immortal."

Killing two people. It wasn't something she'd ever considered being able to do, but Zella had harmed that child who was now a tree and so many others. She had to be stopped.

"I can do it."

Zella didn't deserve to live after those evil deeds. Talia looked into Xavier's deep brown eyes. Even with his face in the mirror, it was hard to picture what he'd look like for real.

"Tell me, Talia. What do you miss most about home?"

She thought for a moment. There were too many things to list.

"My parents most of all. And my horses. And once I get home, I'll have a great appreciation for those working in the castle." The hard work was making Talia strong, but she wouldn't miss scrubbing the floor or cleaning stained clothing.

"And what do you miss most?" she asked. Had his memories faded with time?

A sadness crept across his face. "My parents and my toys."

WHEN THE FOREST CRIES

"Toys?" But he was twenty-two, if she'd done her math right.

"My parents had a ton of toys, and I don't miss playing with them per se, but I miss the idea of them. I lost out on so much when Zella kidnapped me. My childhood was gone, and Bishop's childhood was filled with learning spells. He didn't spend a lot of time outside as I did."

"I understand," she said softly, setting her hand on his. "Oh, can you even feel that?"

"I feel it in my heart." He smiled.

Xavier was an honest man, and together they would make it out of there.

They spent the rest of their time working on the spell that she would have to say to release Xavier. If only she just had to kill Bishop, but they were not so lucky. She needed to say the spell perfectly, and if she did not, then Xavier might die along with Bishop.

It was a lot of pressure to save him, and then they had to save themselves.

Chapter Sixteen

Over the next week, Talia visited Xavier almost every night she could. It was not enough. She craved his company, the only normal in a house of lunatics.

Talia sat on the back step, soaking up the bright sunlight. The last few days she'd been feeding Zella comments about how cozy Charlyn and Bishop looked. Zella's suspicious eyes often followed the pair, but they'd never been doing anything worthwhile to raise her ire. Talia still didn't know how she was gonna set it up so that Zella found them while they were having relations.

Any idea she had would reveal her part in the fiasco. If she sent Zella outside to the shed when they were together, everyone would know.

Zella stuck her head outside the door. "What are you doing on your butt? You have chores to do."

"I'm sorry." Talia stood and wiped off her palms.

"I'm going into town. I'll be back right before dinner."

WHEN THE FOREST CRIES

If only Talia could create a diversion to draw her home early, but she couldn't leave the property, so that was impossible.

The afternoon passed quickly, and soon Talia was busy making dinner in the kitchen. She heard the voices in the living room—a girl's giggle. She stuck her head out and saw a pretty peasant girl sitting on the sofa next to Bishop, an unhappy Charlyn across the room. Zella was in the middle of a story, and the girl laughed.

"Talia," Zella called. "We'll be having another for dinner."

Talia nodded and returned to the kitchen. She considered telling the girl who she really was, but Talia was sure that to this girl, she didn't look like herself.

Zella magicked the food, and Talia spent the dinner listening to coy talk between Bishop and the girl. Seeing the grumpy look on Charlyn's face was satisfying, and in bed that night, she listened to Charlyn toss and turn.

The next day, Bishop was gone, and Charlyn spent the morning grumbling.

SUZI WIELAND

"Change of plans," Zella said, swooping into the room. "It's a harvesting afternoon."

"What?" Charlyn said. "That's not on the schedule."

"I changed the schedule. Here's the map." Zella handed Charlyn a paper, and Charlyn mumbled to Talia to follow her. On the way to the front corner of the yard, they passed Bishop as he headed towards the road.

Charlyn stopped counting and waved him over.

"Where are you going today?" Charlyn smiled, all sickly sweet.

"Errands for my mother. She's trying to cultivate a better relationship with Preston's General Store."

"Preston. Isn't that the girl who was here yesterday?" Her shoulders slumped.

"Yes, it is. I'll see you tonight though." He gave her a wink. "I can't wait."

Charlyn straightened, and Bishop took off.

She looked into the tree. "Come on. Let's get those apples picked."

They climbed the ladders and filled their baskets. Both girls were halfway through their second basket when Zella rushed down the path.

"Stop, stop. What are you doing?" Zella waved her hands in the air.

WHEN THE FOREST CRIES

"What?" Charlyn lowered the basket to the ground, making sure it landed softly.

"You're on the wrong tree." Zella crossed her arms and glared at Charlyn, whose face turned pasty white.

"Wr-wr-wrong tree?" Charlyn swallowed hard and removed the paper from her pocket, and she counted the trees. She gasped.

"Zella, I'm sorry. I didn't mean… Bishop was out here, and we…" She stared at the three baskets on the ground, and Talia let go of the apple she was about to pluck.

"It seems my son has been a bit distracting lately." Zella's voice was tight and controlled, and Charlyn could barely climb down off the ladder. "You have reduced the magic of this tree. I have put so much time and energy into your training, and this is how you repay me? Get to the house," Zella snarled.

Charlyn shuffled away, her head hanging.

"You too, thief," Zella snapped.

Talia followed Zella, and just before Charlyn got inside, Zella called out her name.

"Yes," Charlyn said, turning around.

Zella zipped her hand through the air, the golden powder flying, and a new large tree appeared. Talia's hand swung to cover her gaping mouth.

SUZI WIELAND

Charlyn was gone, given the same fate as Richter's child.

Zella stomped past Talia, and as she passed the tree, she patted the bark. "You'll provide some nice shade."

Talia remained rooted to the ground as Zella paraded up the front steps. At the door, she turned around and motioned to the tree. "It's a beaut, isn't it?"

Then she disappeared inside.

Talia couldn't get the picture of the Charlyn tree out of her head, and under the cover of her scratchy blanket, she stayed up half the night, staring at Charlyn's empty bed. She had worked with Zella for years, and with one wave of her hand, Zella got rid of her.

Talia and Xavier had one—and one chance only— to get out of there, and if they didn't do it right, she would also be a tree.

Talia didn't see Bishop until noon the next day when he showed for lunch with her and Zella.

"What's with the new tree out front?" Bishop asked.

"Are you really that soft in the head?" Zella scoffed. "Didn't you notice someone missing?"

"You turned Charlyn into a tree?" His brows drew up in confusion. "Why?"

WHEN THE FOREST CRIES

"She harvested the wrong tree. Those apples don't have full magic. You think that's funny?"

"Yes," he laughed, but then his face fell serious. "I mean no." He could only hold a straight face for a few moments and burst out laughing again. "Will you find another apprentice?"

"It's so much work for so little benefit. The thief will be around for about three years, so I don't know. You'll have to pick up the slack though."

"Great, now I'm paying for her mistake." He scowled at Talia as if she'd been the one to turn Charlyn into a tree.

"Hard work is good for the soul, my dear." Zella narrowed her eyes at her son, but she said it lovingly.

They didn't care one bit for the poor girl who was now a tree. She was dispensable; everyone was dispensable.

"You and the thief can finish the other tree, and I can handle the processing myself. So you're off the hook for this time."

"Thanks, Mother." He grinned at Talia. "That sounds fun."

She spent the time working with Bishop, and it went much faster than with Charlyn. Thanks to his magic.

That evening, Talia crept into Bishop's room with the mirror. Xavier looked at her with his sympathetic eyes.

"I'm sorry," he said.

"It's not as if I was friends with her, and she didn't even fancy me. But she didn't deserve it." The heaviness weighed Talia down. Charlyn was nothing to Zella and Bishop.

"I don't mean to sound crass," Xavier said hesitantly, "but at least it's one last complication."

"I know." Charlyn had treated her badly, but Talia still felt guilty.

"So are you ready? Whatever day Zella goes to town, we'll start it all?"

"I'm ready." It was now or never, and she hoped that it wouldn't be too long before Zella left the house.

Chapter Seventeen

For two excruciating days, Talia waited for Zella to leave, but she didn't decide to go into town until the third day.

"I'll be back before dinner," Zella said. "Have dinner ready by six."

"Yes, ma'am." Talia's pulse was roaring, and she watched Zella stroll down the path to the road. She remained at the window for another half hour, waiting to see if Zella would return, but she didn't.

Talia snuck to the kitchen to retrieve the knife. Xavier better be right about this because they would both lose their lives if this didn't work. Bishop would die, and Talia would become a tree...

Or worse.

She held the recently sharpened knife in her hand and practiced the words of the spell. It was up to her now. Xavier had done everything he could to prepare her, and both their lives depended on her.

SUZI WIELAND

She took a deep breath and brought the knife out to the woodshed and headed for the office door. This was the easy part.

"Bishop?" Talia knocked, and he yelled to come in. She tugged down her shirt to show off a bit more skin, although the move probably wasn't necessary.

She swung the door open and gave him a smile. "I've been waiting forever for your mother to leave." She jiggled her chest lightly, and his gaze dropped.

"What? Why?" He eyed her suspiciously.

"Silly boy. Now that Charlyn is gone, we can be together. I don't share my men." She winked at him, and his mouth dropped.

This next step would be a bit harder.

She slunk up to him and wrapped her arms around his shoulders and laid a kiss on his lips. He stuck his tongue down her throat, practically choking her, and she pulled back.

"I've been waiting to get a glimpse of these." He groped her breasts over her dress, and she held back her cringe.

Then she grabbed his hand. "Nope. Not here." Blood on Zella's desk would definitely tip her off. "Remember when you made love to that girl in the shed."

"Which girl?"

WHEN THE FOREST CRIES

Talia sighed internally. There were lots of girls he took to the woodshed.

"The one I saw you rolling over the barrel. I've never been able to get that idea out of my head. You don't know how long I've waited to try it out."

"Let's go." He tugged on her hand and dragged her out of the office. They passed a mirror on the way, but Bishop wasn't facing it. She caught a glimpse of Xavier's black hair and hoped he was ready.

Outside in the woodshed, she shut the door. Bishop didn't know it, but she'd left a few buckets of water and towels in the corner. Neither she nor Xavier knew what would happen to the blood Bishop bled before she said the spell.

Bishop hopped across the floor, removing his shoes, then his shirt. In twenty seconds, he'd removed all his clothes.

"There's the barrel." He rolled it into the middle of the shed.

"Your mother is gone all afternoon. We've got plenty of time." She rolled the barrel away with her foot. "Sit down."

He sat down and looked like a dog about to get a bone. She slowly unbuttoned the top of her dress and let it slip to the ground. At least she still had on her underdress.

Bishop handled himself, and Talia blushed. Was Xavier as embarrassed as she was?

"Close your eyes," she said and stepped behind him to grab the knife. She laid it down behind him. "I want you to wait until I get it all off before you look."

Bishop rubbed his hands together excitedly. Her own were clammy. She was about to take a life.

Instead of concentrating on that part, she thought about how Xavier would gain his life back.

"Are you undressed yet?" he asked.

"In just a moment." She picked up her dress and let it thump to the ground so he thought she was removing her underclothes.

"You sit still, and I'll take care of everything." She leaned down to kiss him from behind to give herself a few more seconds.

Her fingers grasped the handle, and she brought it out, keeping her lips on his cheek. Then she pushed back from him and raised her hand.

The knife plunged into his chest, and he screamed. Blood squirted her face, and she squeezed her eyes shut. He kept yelling, and she jerked the knife out and stuck him again and again.

The spell. She had to say the spell.

WHEN THE FOREST CRIES

She recited the four lines out loud as Bishop grasped for the knife. He was too weak though to seize it.

She recited the four lines as Bishop's breaths grew ragged, and he tried to speak.

She recited the four lines and reached for his wrist. He tried to fight her, but his strength was almost gone.

She recited the four lines and watched his head drop back, his eyes glassy.

She recited the four lines as the body beneath her trembled and changed.

She recited the four lines one last time.

Chapter Eighteen

A naked Xavier lay beneath her, his eyes wide open, but she didn't dare breathe, unsure if this was real or if it was another illusion.

"Xavier," Talia said tentatively. Blood covered the floor, but his body was unharmed, and Bishop was gone.

He reached out his hand, and she met his with hers. He shot up and wrapped his arms around her. "You did it. You saved me." He hugged her so tightly she couldn't breathe, but she didn't dare complain.

After a long embrace, she stepped back, and he took her hand. He was even more handsome in person, with his broad shoulders and lovely smile. She made sure to keep her eyes high though.

"I can't believe I'm actually here with you." He squeezed her hand and looked her over. His mouth dropped, and he suddenly spun her around. "I'm so sorry," he gushed.

Talia almost laughed at his embarrassment.

WHEN THE FOREST CRIES

She turned away, and he scrambled to get Bishop's clothes on, which luckily hadn't been stained by any blood, and she put her other dress on over her undergarments.

Once he finished, he held her in his arms once again. "I'll never be able to thank you. Ever."

She wanted to stay in his protective arms, but a dread lingered in her heart. "We're not done yet."

"You're right. Let's go see if we can find those spells and get ready. We won't have much time once she sees me." He smiled softly. "I can't believe this is happening."

They hugged one more time and strode hand-in-hand back to the house. The spell book was waiting in the office, and Xavier sat down to skim the hundreds and hundreds of pages to look for the binding spell and a masking spell.

Talia waited by the front window, on the lookout for Zella. It wasn't as if she could help anyway; the words were still gibberish to her. At least she'd been able to enter the room since Bishop had dropped the protection spell from the door.

"I found the binding spell," he yelled. "Just give me a minute."

SUZI WIELAND

She waited, her body tense, until he came out and showed her the page. "I wrote it out so you could read it too. In case something happens to me."

"Nothing will happen to you." It couldn't. Not now that they'd come so far.

"It won't." He agreed and thumbed through the book. He stopped on a few pages and wrote down a few words. "Now let's go to the tower to make the potion. The masking spell is not too difficult and will only require powder."

"How do you know where to go?"

He chuckled. "I've been watching what's been going on in the tower for years. I know where each and every ingredient is kept."

"Oh, fantastic." She bowed her head. "I hope we don't have to go all the way to the top. That walk tired me out the last time I did it."

He laughed again. "Don't worry. It's the fourth floor."

Inside the room, she stared in amazement at the shelves filled with ingredients. Xavier gathered everything he needed and carried the bottles downstairs to the third floor.

She watched him measure out everything, double and triple checking the recipe. When he finished, he held up the bowl.

WHEN THE FOREST CRIES

"Now. This might go fast. If she knows it's not Bishop, we'll have to do the spell right away, but if she doesn't, I'd rather do it when she's not paying attention. If you're talking to her, I'll say the words quietly behind her."

The pressure was on. They could both lose their lives, but she wouldn't give up without a fight. She'd come too far. She wanted this to be done.

"What's the first thing you'll do when you get home?" Talia asked.

"Hug my parents and find my little brother. The last time I saw him, he was two."

"Me too. Except I don't have a younger sister." She smiled.

"Let's go to the house." He grabbed her hand and squeezed tightly.

Everything will be fine. She repeated those words in her head several times, praying they would be true.

Chapter Nineteen

Talia almost cut off her finger when she was chopping vegetables in the kitchen. She had to settle down, or Zella would know something was wrong. Of course, that was if she didn't notice Bishop had changed.

"She's coming. I'm going to the office." Xavier rushed over and gave Talia a hug. Then he disappeared out the doorway.

He had his half of the potion with him. If Zella realized he wasn't Bishop, then Talia would have to do the spell. The one with Bishop went well, and hopefully this one would too.

As soon as Zella came in the front door, Talia stepped out of the kitchen. "Dinner will be ready within five minutes."

That was Xavier's cue, and he opened the office door. He was close enough to throw the potion and say the spell if he needed to.

Talia held her breath.

WHEN THE FOREST CRIES

"Mother, you're back. I must talk to you about something."

She glanced at him and smiled. "At dinner. I need to clean up." She marched towards the steps, and Talia could barely contain her smile. It was working.

As soon as Zella disappeared, Xavier gave her a grin. "We can do this," he mouthed and motioned for her to return to the kitchen.

Talia finished setting the table, and Xavier got a bottle of wine out. His hand shook when he poured the glass for his *mother*.

"We can do this," she repeated quietly and returned to gathering the food. Xavier sat down.

Zella swooped into the room. "Is dinner ready, thief?" She waited for Talia to nod and took her seat. "Now what was it you wanted to tell me, Bishop dear?"

"It can wait a moment." He laughed. "First you need to magick our food."

"Won't you be doing your own?" She gave him a quizzical look.

"No. Your food tastes so much better. Please do mine too."

Zella laughed and walked to the plates on the counter. She swished her hand, and her food and Xavier's changed.

SUZI WIELAND

"Wait," Talia said, grabbing her wrist. "I hope this dinner is up to your standards."

"What are you doing, you ninny?" Zella jerked away. Behind her, Xavier was saying the lines to the spell, and he tossed the dry potion into the air. A few specks caught in Zella's hair, but most of them floated to the floor.

"Don't touch me again." Zella spun around, and luckily, Xavier was halfway to his seat. They didn't know if the binding spell had worked though.

Xavier was probably right that they needed to disarm Zella before killing her, just in case she was able to escape before death arrived.

Zella returned to the table and sat, and Talia served the plates of food.

"So, now tell me your big news," Zella said, stuffing a glob of mashed potatoes into her mouth.

"Sixteen years ago," Xavier started, "you took something away from me, and now I can finally repay the favor."

"What's that?" Zella asked, not recognizing the danger she was in. Talia wasn't sure what he was waiting for. They needed to kill her, but it seemed as if he was...

WHEN THE FOREST CRIES

Oh no. He was about to tell her who he was. That would give her time to fight back, and they didn't know if the binding spell worked or not.

Xavier, don't. She sent him the thought, but it didn't work.

"Sixteen years ago you stole my life and gave it to your son."

Zella choked on her wine, her eyes becoming wide orbs. "No," she whispered. "Xavier?"

"Yes, it's me."

"It's impossible. I killed you."

"No, you didn't. You trapped me in my body with your son. You made me become a spectator as he took over my body and my life."

"Where's Bishop?" she growled.

"He's where he should've been sixteen years ago. Dead!"

"No!" Zella screamed. She raised her hand in the air and snapped, but nothing happened. She snapped again, with no results. She stared down and wiggled her fingers. She tried once more, but nothing. Then she waved her hand.

"It's called a binding potion," Xavier spat. "I'm sure you know how it works."

SUZI WIELAND

"You bastard." Zella squirmed in her seat, but all she could do was move her body a few inches back and forth and wave her arms. "What have you done to me?"

"An immobility spell. I slipped it into your wine." Xavier grinned, a dangerous gleam in his eye. He'd made more than the binding spell in the tower. This wasn't what they'd talked about.

"Xavier," Talia said, but he ignored her.

"For sixteen long years, I was stuck with the body of an ungrateful, lazy boor who held no respect for anybody. Not even you. I watched you kill people without a second thought. I saw it all, and now it's your turn to suffer." He slid out a large cleaver from under his seat.

Zella trembled as he held it in the air and ran his fingers down the side of the blade. "How do you think it'll feel to lose the parts of you that caused so much damage to so many people?"

"Xavier, don't," Talia pleaded. She wanted Zella dead, but they couldn't torture her. They'd be no better than she was.

"Listen to the thief," Zella whimpered.

"Her name is Talia, and you will say it with respect. Talia." He waved the cleaver close to her exposed neck. "Say it!"

"Talia," Zella cried.

WHEN THE FOREST CRIES

Xavier rose from his seat. "Say your goodbyes to this world." He raised the cleaver high above Zella's wrist. Talia couldn't watch. She squeezed her eyes shut.

The cleaver slammed into the table, but Zella didn't scream. Xavier stood beside her with a smirk on his face. He wrinkled his nose and nodded to Zella. "She peed herself."

"What are you doing?" Talia whispered.

"Death is too good for her." He waved his hand in the air, showering Zella with the powder he'd mixed in the tower.

Suddenly, Zella was a tree, growing in the middle of the kitchen, stretching through the ceiling into the next floor. The cracked and crumbling ceiling rained down on them, and Talia backed away, covering her head.

When everything stilled, Talia rubbed her hand over the scratchy bark of the tree filling the room. "Is she really gone?"

"She will be. There is one last step." Xavier leaned against the counter and closed his eyes.

Talia wrapped her arms around his waist and leaned into his shoulder. "Thank you for not torturing her."

"I wanted to," he choked out. "So badly. But I knew I couldn't live with myself if I did that to her."

116

"What's the last step?" she asked.

"We have a fire. And then we can go home." His face showed a weariness that Talia felt in her bones.

"Then let's go home."

Chapter Twenty

Xavier ran upstairs and started a fire in the room above the kitchen. Then he came downstairs and set several more. Just to be sure, he lit up a few blazes in the parlor too.

They stepped outside together, hand-in-hand, and Talia gasped. Dozens and dozens of dazed and confused people milled around the yard. Adults and children both. The trees were... gone. Almost all of them.

"They were all people she'd taken?" Talia almost cried. So many lives stolen. So many families ruined. "Did you know?"

"Yes." He stared at them, a deep sadness in his voice. "And yes. I said a spell to let them go. I saw her do it once, years ago."

Talia had been the lucky one, only gone for a short time, but there were countless others like Xavier. Talia wanted to get home and see her family, so she couldn't imagine what he felt inside.

SUZI WIELAND

"Let's go." She tugged on his arm, and they made their way down the path away from the growing inferno. Several of the people stared at the burning house.

"Talia," a woman called from the crowd. Talia spun around. Charlyn was rushing towards her. Oh no—Charlyn would hurt her. It would start all over again. Talia backed up into Xavier's arms.

Charlyn ran to her. "Thank you so much. I don't know what you did, but you freed me. You freed us all."

"You were her prisoner too?" Had Zella kidnapped Charlyn?

"Everybody was her prisoner. Even Bishop." Her eyes brightened. "Have you seen him?"

The guilt wallowed inside. Bishop's death was necessary, but she wouldn't feel the pain over it. He was as nasty as his mother.

"He's gone."

"Oh." Tears misted Charlyn's eyes. "Whatever you did, thank you from the bottom of my heart." Charlyn gave her a lingering hug and stepped back. Talia wouldn't tell her that she'd meant nothing to Bishop. Her life would be better without that knowledge.

"Goodbye," Charlyn whispered and wandered off. She stopped at the little boy, Terrence, Richter's son.

WHEN THE FOREST CRIES

She knelt on the ground and took his hand. His scared eyes stared at her, but as she spoke, his body seemed to relax.

"She'll help him, won't she?" Talia asked.

Xavier wound his arm around Talia's waist. "I think she was good underneath, but she was forced into this apprenticeship, and being around the evil changed her. I know she fought it, but it was hard."

Most of the people from the yard were adults, but a few dazed children roamed around. One man and child hugged each other tightly, a family reunited.

Xavier took Talia's hand and led her down the path. "Somebody is about to have an enormous mess to deal with."

Talia stopped once again. "We can't leave them. There are children out there. Kids who don't know how to get home. Some people who may have been stolen from other towns. Who knows how old some of these people were when they disappeared or where they disappeared from."

She had to do something.

Talia clapped her hands loudly. "Excuse me, everybody."

The noise level lowered slightly but not completely. Not until Xavier let out a loud whistle.

SUZI WIELAND

"Anybody here who needs help getting home, please come with me. I'm returning to the castle where the king and queen will help us. Just follow me and Xavier."

"You will make a proper queen someday," Xavier said, and Talia felt the pride emanating from his eyes.

They started the slow procession through the town. People exited their homes to watch what was going on, and by the time they ended up at the castle, the line had grown even longer. A few reunions had happened along the way, and the crowd buzzed with energy.

"Princess," someone called, and in seconds, bodies surrounded her, hugging her, trying to tug her away from Xavier, but she didn't let go. Everybody was asking a million questions, and she could barely answer them.

"Talia," a strong voice said. She spun around and saw her mother, tears in her eyes. She let go of Xavier's hand and flew into her mother's arms. Not long after, her father joined in, embracing them tightly.

The story came out in bits and pieces, and her father mobilized a crew to deal with the lost souls.

Finally, she was able to lead her parents to the man who had rescued her. He stood tall with a grand smile on his face.

WHEN THE FOREST CRIES

"Mother, Father, this is Xavier, the man I told you about."

"Thank you, kind sir. Thank you for saving my daughter." Talia's mother threw her arms around Xavier, and he accepted the hug.

"Thank you, but it is your daughter who saved me." Xavier stared at Talia with gratitude, and she blushed. "And it's a pleasure to meet you, Your Highness." Xavier bowed to her mother and father. "And Your Majesty."

"Xavier," the king said, studying Xavier curiously. "What is your last name, and where do you hail from?"

"Beck. Xavier Beck. Of Larvik."

The king's smile grew. "I knew your face seemed familiar. My dear," he said, turning to the queen. "Xavier is the son of King Arvid and Queen Haley."

Talia gasped. "He's a prince?" Nobody paid her any attention though.

The queen grasped Xavier's hands, tears filling her eyes. "Then this is a double blessing for us today."

"You know my family, sir?" Xavier's face swung between Talia's parents.

The king smiled gently. "When Talia was four, and you were five, we took a trip to Larvik."

"We did?" Talia had no recollection of that trip and didn't remember anybody talking about it ever.

SUZI WIELAND

"You two played together on the castle grounds for hours for four whole days. You were fast friends, and we were saddened when we heard of your disappearance a year later." The king laid his arm on Talia's shoulders. "My dear, meet Prince Xavier Beck of Larvik."

"A prince?" Talia could hardly process everything. "You never told me."

"It didn't seem important." He shrugged.

"Radcliff," the king called, and his steward ran up. "We need to prepare for a trip to Larvik for the four of us." He turned to Xavier. "We'll leave as soon as everything is ready. I'm sure you want to get home."

"That means a lot to me, Your Majesty. Thank you." Xavier nodded graciously.

"Why don't you two go get cleaned up, and we'll get something to eat. In a few hours, we'll begin our trip." The king patted Xavier on the back and rushed off after Radcliff.

Talia spun around to face Xavier. "I can't believe you're a prince."

"And you're a princess," he said, his gaze growing intense.

"That's mighty convenient." Talia wrapped her arms around his neck.

WHEN THE FOREST CRIES

"It is," he agreed, tugging her close. He kissed her softly, tenderly, and Talia knew from then on there was no place she'd rather be.

The End

Acknowledgments

Thank you to Karen Sanders for catching a lot of those stupid little mistakes that are so easy to miss.

And thank you to all my Beta Peeps friends for being such an awesome group: Cassie Mae, Jade Hart, Jennie Bennett, Jenny Morris, Jessica Salyer, Kelley Lynn, Lizzy Charles, Rachel Schieffelbein, and Theresa Paolo. I'm happy to still call you all my friends and thankful for your help and support along the way!

About the Author

Reading has always been a big part of Suzi's life. She even won the most-pages-read award a few times in her junior high English class, many years ago. She started several writing projects as a kid but never actually finished anything, and then she took a big break from writing that lasted well into adulthood.

She's written in a variety of genres, including horror, suspense, and women's fiction, and has even dipped into fantasy slightly with her fairy tale retellings. She also writes young adult stories under the name Suzi Drew.

Her non-writing life includes her family and friends, her sweet and fluffy dog, and an awesome job editing fiction with some of her writer friends. (Oh wait, that's still a part of writing. Seems she can't get away from the written word!)

To find out more about Suzi,
go to SuziWieland.com

Also by Suzi Wieland

<u>Thriller Novels</u>
Black Diamond Dogs

<u>Horror Novels</u>
House of Desire

<u>Horror and Suspense Novellas/Short Stories</u>
Shallow Depths
(Un)lucky Thirteen
Long-Term Effects
The Silent Treatment
A Story to Tell
Panne Dora Pass

Twisted Twins Series
Glenda and Gus
Two for the Price of One
A Hard Split

<u>Fairy Tale Novellas</u>
The Down the Twisted Path Series
The Whole Story
An Unwanted Life
Killing Rosie
The Perfect Meal
When the Forest Cries
In the Queen's Dark Light

Please visit SuziWieland.com
for more information.

Milton Keynes UK
Ingram Content Group UK Ltd.
UKHW030951261124
451585UK00001B/47